The Tell Tale
Collection

The Tell Tale
Collection

Maeve
Devoy

Ballpoint Press

For Valerie

Published in 2013 by Ballpoint Press
4 Wyndham Park, Bray, Co Wicklow, Republic of Ireland.
Telephone: 086 8217631
Email: ballpointpress1@gmail.com

ISBN 978-0-9572072-5-7

Book design and production by Elly Design

Printed and bound by GraphyCems

~ CONTENTS ~

~ INTRODUCTION ~

OVER THE space of one summer and half an autumn, I drove all over Ireland and interviewed 15 people with my dictaphone and my notebook.

I asked them about their lives, their families, their friends, their fears and their surroundings. They were born in different decades from the 1920s right up to the turn of the century.

I hope their tales weave a rich tapestry of Ireland down through the years as its people faced up to the things that they could not change in society and tried to balance them against those that they could.

I wanted to use their stories as a foundation for my stories and I would like to thank them for their sincerity. I have changed certain dates, events, relationships and every name to disguise their identities and allow what is my interpretation of their lives.

Maeve Devoy
May 2013

1 A Time To Sing

THEY WEREN'T just stories, they were relics. They were over 2,000 years old and Fionn's mother was singing them to the familiar air. The water rippling in the kitchen sink and her chest rising to the muddy beat in her lungs. She shut her eyes while the ancient Irish words passed through her, there was never any need to translate the soul.

It was sacred.

It was Sean Nos and her voice stood alone with its nasally ornamentation, dramatic pauses and no accompaniment, no loud and no soft. She was always singing bits and pieces of the same song; an old woman in the Kerry mountains had taught her how to sing it when she was a young girl.

It was an important part of her tradition and Fionn's father had spent his entire life collecting Irish music, trying to save what he could of those words. He travelled all over the country with his work. He organised sessions and fleadhs and drove down to Kerry to listen to that weathered lady by the lake outside her house.

She was a legend.

She told Fionn's father about a session that was on later that evening. He went and heard Fionn's mother singing a tragic tune and he was captivated by her gentle tone. He moved down south to be with her and to revel in the tradition he loved.

He never strayed too far from the form. He always sang a song from start to finish. Without fail, he would sing. He would give anything a go, the fiddle or the banjo. He played the flute and the tin whistle in the car and it annoyed the hell out of Fionn. His father was quite happy to sit and play in his own little world while his mother shopped for hours on end.

Fionn liked to be out exploring, hacking away at the burly nettles and disappearing for hours on his quests to the park and down the busy roads. He was born in the middle of his eight brothers and sisters; he had red hair and freckles and dressed in hand-me-downs.

He read folklore and his mother helped him understand the stories, the epic sagas, Tir Na Nog and the children that were turned into swans for 900 years. He lived in those books and wore out his shoes in a week hopping fences, building carts and growing up. He used to visit the remains of the overgrown slaughterhouse that was buried behind the town. There were skulls and bones everywhere and Fionn used to take them home to examine them and pretend they were the victims of his hallucinatory war.

He played GAA and hurling and his parents kept signing him up for music lessons. He kept picking up the tin whistle and putting it down. He wasn't into it – he wasn't like his sisters. He never listened to music or studied it in secondary school.

They entered competitions, the provincials and the All Irelands. They had 30 medals between them but Fionn didn't put too much thought into what he wanted to do or be as he went to the summer fleadh with his family. He sat in the dark chamber of a sullen pub and listened to a crumpled man sing that song his parents loved. For the first time he was startled. He'd never heard it sung in such a way, in such a primal shape of sadness.

It dragged Fionn way down into the murky depths of the rhythm writhing over him and it soaked that saggy-faced man through and through. His eyes were closed and he let it go, let it go until the thunder on his tongue tore Fionn from his stool and left him clapping and his eyes watering, blinking.

That man hadn't sung the song particularly well but he'd sung it with what was in him and Fionn was so struck that he wanted to try it. He started singing with his father and to himself in the shower or in the garden. He asked his father to write down the words and he learnt them off but kept them to himself. His father was the one that entered him into the competition a month later.

Fionn wished he hadn't.

He was standing outside a thatched pub with a large crowd and the grass was slipping and dithering beneath his leather boot. He forgot all of the words and let his nerves trickle down his throat and guzzle the loose air from his lungs.

He quivered.

He couldn't lower his eyelids with the fear. He scraped at the memory of the notes in his head and nothing came out but a cough. He swore he would never do it again and went home to study engineering in the autumn.

He was 18.

He hung up his musical muscles and the silence locked its bulky chain around his failure. He never spoke of it. He strangled it and played sports instead. He was in college for three years, equipping himself for the industry and the real world and he got a job as soon as he graduated.

He worked for a company doing quality control and graphic design and if anybody in there was doing their job properly, they would have realised that Fionn didn't know what was going on. He didn't get the point behind those buttoned-up windows and the people he worked with never explained anything to him. He was just doing what he presumed they expected him to do and avoiding the computers for the year.

❀ ❀ ❀

He went back to college to get a masters in computer programming and met his wife Una there. She was locking up her bicycle beside his in a hurry to get to class. Fionn went with her to some lecture that made very little sense and he was taken by the wizardry of the chiming bells in her voice.

She was pretty too.

She let Fionn take her hand when they fed the ducks and when he dared, he kissed her and closed his eyes to listen to the rhyme in her words. She never noticed it herself. She wasn't into music. She liked reading. She read the news out loud to Fionn and the harmony in her voice was the only secret Fionn had from her.

He never let her go.

They were together a year when he asked her to marry him. She said yes and he wasn't one bit nervous under the marquee on their wedding day. Her steps were in time with the lilt in his limbs and the session went on all night long. His family were at him to sing them a song and they wouldn't take no for an answer. He had it in him, they said, it was flooding through his veins and he had to dig up the nerve to do it.

So he did it.

He sang that old tune with his parents and held onto Una with the ivy of his eyes. He was trundling through the verses and catching himself like a sleeve or a hanky on the notes he was unsure of. She smiled and blew him away onto the next and then, the song was over.

He stood down.

In life, he got a good job as an engineer. He was getting by, paying the mortgage and paddling towards any bit of light or interest that broke up the boredom of his office. His father asked him if he would do him a favour. There was a fog settling over the tradition of Sean Nos and the local newspaper wanted an article written about it.

Fionn was happy to write it.

He had a son on the way and he'd been thinking a lot about his days as a young boy at the fleadh. He went with his family every summer. He saw the jigs, the reels, the sweat pumping out of the musicians and the feet bruising the floorboards while the tempo flushed away the walls of the day and into the night. There were bards, bodhrans, dancers and drunks that were polite and they were there every year. There was no better feeling or place Fionn would rather have been than the fleadh and it was different every time, in every place. In every person there was a verse and it was Fionn's truth.

He had to sing.

He had to use what his parents had given him and dredge up new airs, new sounds from inside of him and hum, whistle and pipe out his lungs to Una and his son. He couldn't stop. He bumped into a fiddler he knew from somewhere, this fleadh or that fleadh and they got to talking over a couple of whiskeys one night. Fionn sang his parents song his own way and loosened his own timbre into it.

The fiddler loved it.

They started working together and creating their own rendition of their traditions. They scribbled out the lines between their timings and tempo and merged their highs and their lows.

The company Fionn was working for downsized and let him go and he spent his time unravelling his memories from his joints. He churned what was old into something very unique and orchestrated the cellos, adapted the melodies, the pictures and the story he took from the Book of Leinster.

It was perfect.

It was An Tain.

It was about a shift in borders, a movement in the people and Queen Maedhbh, manipulating armies of men and thrones of kings and promising wealth she had no intention of giving for the brown bull. She sent a warrior every day to Cuchulainn's sword and he struck every one of them down until she was defeated and he was bound to a stone to die standing and proud. It was the greatest story of them all and it gave Fionn's audience a common ground to stand upon that following spring.

He stacked the amps up high on the church's altar and figured out the acoustics. He needed to absorb the space. Otherwise, the whole damn thing would fall flat and everything he'd been working for would disintegrate. He didn't want that. He was doing something no one had ever done before and he'd forgotten the fear, the bum note.

He would sing until he spluttered out and washed up out of the silence, out of metre and form and convention. He put his hands behind his back and signalled for the fiddle to hail and wail.

It was time.

He shut eyes and felt it, followed it and walked it through forests, scooted it across ravines to dive right into it and when the words started slipping like ice into summer, he splashed them with thrills and let them break against his throat and set him free.

2 Eagles In The Chicken Coop

VERA HAD never imagined life without her big sister, Sharon. She was the gentle gale that blew out the candles before they slept and said goodnight. She was the quiet queen of bedtime monsters and shaking rafters in the wild, wild wind. She was the kind hand that slept, warm and sound, in Vera's.

They peddled and played in the park together. They carried their mother's groceries back from Meath Street. They ferried buckets of water up and down the trampled wood of the crying staircase.

They sat side by side in the circle of children and knotted their knees into one. They linked arms and little thumbs while looking dead into their mother's shining eyes. They listened carefully. Their mother didn't have energy to shout. She would tell them a story about one day when there was this eagle flying over a barn. He dropped an egg into the nest of a farmyard chicken and the egg cracked but still hatched.

The baby eagle grew up on the farm walking like a chicken, squawking like a chicken and looking up at the eagles in the sky. He died a chicken because that's what he thought he was and it was tough. But it was life. They too would get no favours from fate. They knew better than anyone where they were coming from.

The tenement walls were tipping over and charred from the years of neglect that had been in them. There were seven families living there on three different floors. There were over 30 children laughing and crying in the dark and damp of those clustered rooms. There was no running water. There were two toilets outside with the concrete and the coal box, the crisscrossing of their clotheslines and their lifetimes. There were two taps but if the one in the yard was running, the other on the landing wouldn't work.

Those people got nothing easy or free or fair and they were the jokers, the fighters, the charmers and the shiver at dawn in that dirty old town. For all that they were brilliant neighbours. They looked out for one another and their children. They never let anyone go short. They swapped their evening papers in the hallway at eight o'clock on the dot. They returned every cup of sugar, every favour and that was the thing about that house, none of those people had ever thought they were badly off.

They were heroes.

Her parents never had any money either. Vera's father had been in and out of work all his life. He never had any luck. He helped a farmer sell pigs at the market once a week. He might have seen a shilling or a penny on a good day.

He was a gentleman.

He never drank.

He stood by every hand he shook and never fought or had a minute for the St. Vincent de Paul. Vera's mother wouldn't have it. They would have insisted she sell the pretty pieces from her wedding and they were all she had apart from tatters, potatoes and a niece that called round every Sunday for lunch.

She would leave a shilling or a sixpence on the mantle by the spotless mirror and nothing was ever said about it. Vera's mother swept it under the hard face of her pride. She'd spent her entire life scrimping and saving and she had eight hungry mouths to feed, they came first. She slept in the kitchen with Vera's father, the baby, the cot and the gas cooker. She split the box room in half for the children.

She went without.

Vera had witnessed the dark holes dig into the creases of her mother's face and watched as her skin drew tighter, her hair went whiter as it lost the red hue of her youth. Yeh, she'd been a young one once. She'd been sweet on the fellas and the fair. Her hopes and her dreams had been real too. But she always said, when poverty comes in the window, love goes out the door and Vera believed her.

Vera was the same little growl of flame with her curls the colour of strawberries in June. She knew she didn't want to end up like her mother and neither did Sharon. They would have to speak up and spit it out or they would get nothing. The city couldn't suffer another sorry tale. They had to work. Vera's mother had told them from the start, the boys needed to stay in school and get an education. The girls would get married and looked after.

Sharon was first.

She was four years older than Vera and working as a seamstress. They were still carrying the buckets of water, the groceries and talking. Sharon told Vera there wasn't anything to be afraid of, that it wouldn't be so bad when it was her turn – and it wasn't. Vera was 14 when her mother got her an apprenticeship in the boxmill.

It was a trade.

Vera made Black Magic boxes and worked from eight in the morning until six in the evening. She cut and glued the cardboard, folded the corners and tied the bows. The workers sang their songs in their rows about the old times and Vera whistled the old melodies until the death of each new day.

Sharon was the bravest. She upped and left like a warm breath on the glass of a cool morning. A little blur and she was gone. She organised it all on her own. She signed the contract, took the £10 the New Zealand government had paid her to go. She bought a suitcase with the money and packed her clothes. She told her family the same week. They all went to see her off and she waved goodbye from the deck until the clouds drifted over and blew her out.

Vera didn't know why Sharon did it, how she ever went so far on her own. She'd seen the sadness creep into Sharon's face on the grey mornings and she didn't know what it was or where it had come from, but it had aged the spirit in Sharon's step before she left.

Vera's mother imitated the grey stone of her own grave without Sharon. There was nothing Vera could do to console her. One lost a daughter and the other a sister and a friend. Vera never thought she would see Sharon again. Her father hid it better. He had a high colour in his cheeks and he said he was happy for Sharon.

Vera got up in the mornings missing her. She leaned into the empty space of Sharon's shape in the frosty mattress but her fingers never found what they longed for. She went to work and the hops in the evening thinking of Sharon. She had no one to talk to and she kept the letters Sharon wrote once a month, tied and bound to the empty space of her drawer.

She kept them safe and read them whenever there was an ache in her heart. She unfolded them gently and let the words kindle a candle below the memory of her sister's face. Sharon was settled and after a month on the boat to New Zealand, she had a job and a little apartment in the city. She was making her way and Vera was doing the same damn thing, only it was still carrying those buckets of water and those bags of groceries.

She remembers looking up from the boxes in front of her one

morning in work to see a girl she had gone to school with crossing the factory floor and stepping into the office.

An office worker! Vera bit her tongue. She was just as good as that girl in school. She twisted and burned and went home to lug herself up, up and up the old staircase that had begun to mock her with the moon bleeding bright beyond the window and the night.

Something had risen up inside of Vera and pulled itself up from the oil of her tears. She didn't know what it was. But she knew she was going to have to do more than others if she was going to smother it.

She opened her eyes.

She started night classes and learnt how to type and write shorthand in 1963. The boxmill closed down. It was too expensive to make boxes by hand and Vera didn't get the chance to finish her apprenticeship. She was lucky. She sat an exam and got a job in the civil service as a punch-card operator. She was very good at it. It was at the very beginning of computers and the whole building was filled up with machines.

Vera was 21 and she was moving on in many facets of her life. She was getting married to Dermot. She met him at the end of a ladies' choice and thought he was funny. He was the lankiest fella in the room and she couldn't miss him or say 'no' when he asked her up for the next dance. His face went redder than the evening in bloom. He made her laugh and they fell in love of a Sunday night. They went for walks, saved their money and watched every penny that fell into their hands.

Vera's father had been adamant that they had a deposit for a house. She got another job in a restaurant by working nights. She knew what it was worth and Dermot too cleaned windows after working the day as a carpenter. He picked Vera up after her shift on his Honda 50 and drove her home. They carried their lives on that motorbike and never went out.

When they saved enough money for a deposit they got married. Vera's father gave them £100 as a wedding present and it must have been three weeks wages for him at the time. Vera couldn't believe her eyes. Best of all Sharon came home for the wedding and for a couple of weeks, it felt as if she'd never left, as if nothing had changed.

Their mother had been on the corporation list for a house for years and she was 60 when she finally got out of the tenements. She was delighted. She hadn't as much to worry about now that the kids were reared. Two of her boys were working and she could afford to keep the younger ones in school, things were that bit easier for her.

Sharon was speechless and squeezing Vera's hand when she saw the house. She stood back, took in a long breath and drank tea until there was nothing left to say. She held Vera a little longer and tighter than the rest. She went back again. Vera's mother turned that awfully grave colour. But they all knew Sharon had to go and they couldn't ask her to stay.

She had her own little bakery now in New Zealand. She had a home and a family that would be waiting for her by the dock of the bay when she returned. She didn't write to Vera as often. She didn't have time.

Vera had to give up her job in the civil service after she got married. That was the law at the time. She could have done with the money. The mortgage was £19 a month and Dermot was smoking 20 cigarettes a day with the stress. Vera was doing anything she could to make sure she never went back to where she'd come from. She learnt to knit. Her mother taught her how and she was really bad at it in the beginning.

She stitched the lines backwards but kept at it, got better and better and sold cardigans and matinee coats to every mother in the neighbourhood. She sent Aran jumpers to America and wouldn't sit in front of the TV without something in her hands.

She had two more mouths to feed and their house was a bit small for them all out in the middle of nowhere. Vera knew they could do better. She saw a house up for sale with four bedrooms that was qualified for Bed and Breakfast. She figured if they did a bit of that and stepped out of the ashes of where they'd come from they could afford the £99 a month mortgage.

It was tough though. They would get a call from people wanting to stay in the B&B and have to haul the children out of bed for them. The kids slept in the garage for the summer and let strangers lie in their beds. It was what they needed to do and they did it without hesitation. Vera gave birth to her only daughter when she was 32. She'd put on an awful lot weight after having Shauna. She joined Trimmings to get back into shape and the rest, she said, was history.

She lost all of the extra weight after a few months with Trimmings. She applied for a job as a team leader. She would have to watch her 'dese' and 'dose', her 'dis' and 'dat,' the management told her but she had the job. What they said annoyed her. It had unwrapped her skin from the marrow of her being. It wasn't right and she wouldn't let something or someone like that hold her back. She started elocution lessons and trained herself to pronounce her words correctly. In a short time, no one could hold a candle to her at the job.

She liked helping people lose weight and feel better about themselves. She seemed to know what to say to inspire them. Then without much warning, the word filtered through that the company was pulling out of Ireland. They were based in France and they weren't making enough profit to stay. They left the 13 women they had employed behind with their weighing scales and their hopes high and dry.

Vera drove the head of the company to the airport and he wished her the very best of luck. She went back to those 13 women and said to them, honestly and truthfully, if they made a go of it and stuck together, it would change their lives.

❀ ❀ ❀

They were just 13 mothers who happened to be in the same place at the same time; everything was against them. They had two classes each, terrible tempers and no degrees. They pooled two weeks of their wages together. They were all hungry for it to succeed and between them they turned that company around. Vera was the peace-keeper. She kept those women together and looking forward. Vera and Dermot rewrote the weight-loss programme in plain English.

It took off like a rocket and Vera sunk herself into it hand and foot. She always knew what they should do next because she had the vision for it. She recruited more people and more leaders, opening more and more classes every month. There were over 1,000 Trimmings meetings a week and she would think, if this goes well, her family could go on holiday. They could do everything Vera had never let herself dream about before and she never let herself forget where she was from.

She was a long way away from the tenements and it was the coming from that place of nothing that had brought her there. She had three bathrooms and five bedrooms, two dogs and a horse next door. She'd made it. Sharon came back to visit and drink tea, take a walk down the old street, by their old house and they talked about their lives. Sharon said Vera had made it.

The last time they saw each other the rain fell too hard for words. It was their mother's funeral and their father's before that. It wasn't easy to have to say so many goodbyes. Vera had never asked Sharon why she left her to go to New Zealand in all the years.

She had wondered and let it go, let it slip right out of her. Until now.

She ran after the taxi with its yellow and bursting light. It was leaving the length of her driveway and Vera threw her hand against the car window. The taxi braked to a halt. She opened the door and asked Sharon why she did it, how she ever had the courage to go.

Sharon looked surprised and when she stepped out of the car, she pulled Vera close and tight. They hugged for a little eternity. Sharon whispered into Vera's ear that she didn't want to die like that chicken, that eagle and she couldn't have gone on surrendering herself without finding the hue a different horizon. The tenements were turning her skin and dreams to stone and it would have taken more courage for her to stay like Vera.

With that, she took a hold of Vera's hand, warm and perfect in hers. She pointed at the moon like a lighting lantern in the sky and told Vera to look up, to always look up. Up from the platoons of skeleton rooms and creaking stairways, up from the smoky hauntings of the labour and the Liberties, because they were the two eagles that had flown.

3 Life Through The Lens

THE WORLD had gone nuts, completely terrifying. There were men in uniforms pulling other men by the scruff of their collars from their wives and their newborn babies and beating them. They were whooping through the streets showing they meant business – they would fill the cells.

That's how it looked to the people of the nationalist side and they were tired of it. They cordoned off their own ghettos with balaclavas on their heads and guns in their hands. They painted 'Keep Out' on the walls that were left standing. There were bullets flying, people missing and plotting in rooms with lights low and weapons on the table.

It was 1971 and there were armoured cars and soldiers in camouflage with guns in their hands and knives in their holsters. They'd taken another son, another neighbour from the crowded cul de sac of Martin's youth. He was 10 years old. He could just about say that dreaded internment word and close the curtains. He hadn't the nerve for the Troubles.

He was a small boy.

His fondness was for the darkness where he spent most of his time on his own, taking things apart and forgetting how to put them back together. There were tiny disassembled cities and deconstructed pieces of junk all over the kitchen, stairs and hall. He was a curious creature, the youngest of five children and the golden boy of his parents. They didn't mind what he was doing, once he stayed out of the way of the Troubles.

He adored his mother. She took him to half six mass every morning. She enjoyed the company and Martin didn't mind going with her – he liked the smell of the incense.

His father was a bus driver, a trade union man and considered something of a local wise man. The neighbours were forever calling round to see him about letters they needed written and seeking his advice on how to employ politicians to help them. Martin was drawn to their conversations. He didn't like to miss a word when his father spoke.

His father was a man of vision and he had a garage down the road from their house which he filled full of old car parts to sell on. He also had cameras from his own father's interest in films. The reels and reels of film showed all of the family members except martin's granddad – that was because he was on the other side of the lens. Martin had never seen his face but his father said he looked just like him.

His grandfather was an interesting man. He worked on the railways down south with the writer Sean O'Casey. They talked about the unrehearsed stage of existence and their rooms piled high with journals and photographs. Martin admired their ideas. He couldn't get enough of them. He lost days on end trawling through his grandfather's boxes.

His parents bought him a motorbike at an auction that year which he kept in the garage. The bike was a distraction and it kept him busy. It gave his parents a further bit of comfort. They knew he was safe.

On the streets his eyes were wide and watchful but despite claims that it was possible, he could never tell the peoples' faith from their faces. The people were tired looking. Martin listened to their whispers; they were sick of pretending everything was normal when it wasn't.

Martin hadn't opened his curtains for ages. He didn't dare, things had gotten worse. There were tanks and bombs, traps and kidnappings, assassinations and stabbings, torture and gangs. There were ceasefires and massacres, murder and children tripping over rifles.

POK!

That was the sound of the pesky-eyed bullets that had driven Martin up to the very top of the biggest hill in town. He took a pair of binoculars from his father's garage to play army man and to see what the soldiers saw. There was nothing – just holes where the streets used to be. There was death and debris, dust and doom everywhere he looked.

Martin was a typical teenager flirting with the Provisional IRA in school. The older guys had been telling him where to go and when. He was sick of it, wasn't he? They'd seen him on that hill and they'd taken him after school. They put a hood over his head and drove him somewhere with something sticking into his back. They asked him ridiculous questions like who had sent him?

They were testing him.

He passed.

They took the blindfold off and let his eyes warm to the rutted black of the disused building. It was a dismal sort of place. Martin knew it from the railings that hung from its caving walls and he didn't want to see inside of it anymore. He wanted to run. But he did what was best. He kept his mouth shut, did what they said and never went back.

He went further into the maddening shade of his room. They came knocking on his door. Martin was a wobble out in the daylight. He faded into the shadow of the gunmen; the soldiers kept at him. They kept asking him to dig a place to hide their guns in his back garden and they were vulgar when he couldn't do it.

They laughed in derision.

They left.

Martin ran upstairs and went down on his knees while he rocked to and fro. He couldn't scrape their images from his head. They haunted him for two days and then he had to go out. He was getting groceries for his mother down the town. He heard an engine grit its teeth and a group of teenagers came galloping around the corner with stones and grudges.

Martin had to do something. The tension was brawling its way towards him in a ball of smoke and there were four paratroopers hanging from the steely snout of their stripped down jeeps. They were cackling like hyenas. He couldn't be a coward. He carefully placed the plastic bag with his mother's bread and milk in the gutter and picked up a lump of stony shrapnel. It was a peculiar feeling. The troops were trying to tempt him closer to catch him and Martin was trying to get close enough to hit them with a brick.

He hadn't thought of his parents. He hadn't stopped to think at all really. He threw it. He hit one of them in the leg and they chased him down alleys, through gardens and holes in fences.

He ran for his life.

He wasn't too familiar with that part of town and they caught him. They pinned him to the brick wall and started loading bullets into their guns. They were pointing and joking as they arrested Martin and they took him to the station after they'd had their fun.

His father had to come and get him. His parents were disappointed over what happened but Martin promised them that would be the end of it.

He withdrew to the red-lighted gloom of the attic where he'd built his dark room. He took down the model railway his father had crafted from scratch and commandeered the dark space, morning, noon and night. He stayed away from the streets with the soldiers and scoured yards searching for baths, salts, acids and rubber drains.

He connected one sink to another and started taking photographs. He constructed his own enlarger and developed his own pictures, collections and leaning towers of stuff and things. It was his empire and there were days he never left.

He barricaded the hole in the floor to keep the POK! sound of the shooting out. He read encyclopaedias, drew badly and painted madly. Most of all he couldn't stop taking photographs of his family or ever leave the house without his grandfather's camera close to his eye.

By the age of 17, he pestered his parents into buying him his own. He still remembers it, the fusty scent of the soft Russian leather.

He inhaled it.

He mitched from school because of it and hid in his father's garage just poking about. He wanted to keep himself out of sight and out of trouble. The school finally rang his parents to complain about his lack of attendance. What on earth had he been thinking? He was a minor genius according to the IQ test he had done. He couldn't afford to be missing class and for the first time in his life, Martin felt awful.

He started going to art classes to make up for it. He also tried harder at school. He was doing something. He was looking for a way out of the whitewashed asylum of the daily chaos. A tutor told Martin how he could get a grant for art college.

Martin went to live in Belfast when he was accepted. His father shook his hand the day he left. His mother cried.

He'd never been to a dance or had a girlfriend in his life. Suddenly, he was free. He set himself loose from the cover of the darkroom ever so slowly. He made friends and found the booze and the light rooms. He seldom went home. He stayed in the studios working and painting and taking photographs. Word about his work spread and Martin was establishing himself as something of an artist at that point. Every bit of his work was a part of the Troubles.

It was nutty stuff and the currency he got paid in was reputation rather than bank notes. But that wasn't his motivation; he was driven to capture the different layers of the soldiers' scales and scopes. There was no way he could lay it all to rest when he finished his year there and went home. He applied to the London School for Media and brought over his portfolio full of stone throwing for the interview.

He got a letter a few weeks later saying he was in. He was thrilled. London was chaotic and that suited Martin. He had a suitcase and a camera, no plans and no big idea. He loved it there. He drank and smoked Columbian grass and enjoyed the momentary disintegration of the mind. He had flings and affairs with woman who had fantastic bodies and he fell in and out of love too many times and not often enough.

He was devoted to his work. He wanted people to take a walk in his shoes, to carry the bricks he was given and feel the weight of the stone in his soul. The other students didn't like him. They burnt his pictures from the walls and the lecturers were effing and blinding at each other behind unlocked doors. They couldn't agree over his work.

He lived in a council flat for the three years he was in London. He had no job, no money and the poverty finally stifled him into starving when he finished college. He had no choice but to pack up his camera and his suitcase and go home. His parents were delighted. Martin slipped back under the dark rug of his shrunken empire as if he'd never left. He took pictures everywhere he went for his portfolio hoping they might get him into Hampton Bridge. It was the most prestigious art school in London.

The examiners from the Bridge told him they'd seen all of his work and Martin couldn't just take pictures of the Troubles anymore. He had to do something different, something new. He pulled his dark room apart and waded through the boxes and piles of film trying to find something of himself, something other than the Troubles.

But it was like his grandfather's face was his own. Martin wasn't there. He was missing. He went through every photograph but couldn't find the little boy he had once been. In all it took him three years to step out from the shadows and design a seven digit time display that was 16 foot tall. He made it out of red plastic and pvc, corrugated cardboard and glue, light-bulbs that counted up and down and played number games. He hung it from the local art centre back home.

It was so different that it made the television news. There were people taking notice of him and an old man of performance art put in a good word for him at the Bridge.

※　※　※

The examiners finally let him in – that was it. He said goodbye again, shook hands, wiped tears and moved back to London.

He was 27 years old and he had grown into a very serious young man. They never really knew what he was up to in the Bridge. His notes were unintelligible. His work was mad. He was so involved in what he was doing that he was inches away from falling right into the chemical stew he brewed on his own.

The stuff was potent.

He hated doing the projects, the bordered briefs and he built his own computer for his final show. He soldered the chunks of metal and wire and paid £35 for a voice synthesizer and a couple of quid for a gold painted statue of Christ. He cut off its jaw, gave it springs and red LED eyes. He programmed it to talk: 'I'm your lord and master.'

It was a riot.

There was a red light flashing against the shards of the moments he'd shot, the streets, the stones and the soldiers he'd cut up and put back together his own way. They were collages. Martin had struck gold. He was awarded high marks for his particular kind of lunacy and he graduated from the Bridge.

He made a name for himself in the magazines and on the radio. There were people interested in his work and the more popular it got, the more Martin got told what was right for the people see and what was not. The British government censored his work. It was infuriating. He had nowhere to show and no one to care that it was his life they were banning from their halls.

He had to get out of there.

It was corrosive.

He arrived back with 72 collages stuffed into plastic bags. He was penniless. His parents had sold their house to his oldest brother. They didn't think Martin would be back. They didn't think they needed the extra room.

Martin was homeless. He was a bearded wreck and he had to stay with his sister, collect his boxes and his bits and catch a bus down south a few days later.

He got a bed-sit in Dublin city. He spent days in his plywood room with scalpels, microscopes and glue. He went through every picture he'd ever taken and started to see glimpses of himself in the darkest parts. It all made sense. He was never meant to be in anyone's army. He'd been the one shooting the camera, not the gun and that would never change. He kept making collages and cutting up pictures of the world. He let the children gather meteorites instead of stones, the men threw stars and built pyramids.

He pasted himself in.

He was an astronaut, an artist.

He figured that they were all just little pieces of the same mayhem. They were one pretty blur. The city loved the idea. Martin got full-page spreads in the newspapers. His exhibitions were trafficked with people and his work was selling. He could afford a new place with enough space for all his cardboard and troubles. People finally knew his name and let his pictures hang from the walls.

His work was showing all over the country on postcards, mugs and art brochures. There was a buzz about him; he even had a gallery for his work. The town council commissioned him to sculpt a memorial statue up north. They gave him a book with the name of every person that had died in the Troubles for inspiration.

It was a mad, mad thing, the paper was thick as a brick. It was a heavy read. Martin recognised too many names from those pages and pages of short obituaries. He read about the butcher and the librarian, the mother and the secret agents, the friends that had blown themselves up in living rooms with nail bombs. They were all dead and gone to pieces. It knocked Martin sideways. The town thanked him for the sculpture. It was bronze and it trapped the light of the day to save the souls of ones they'd lost.

It's still there.

Martin's parents had passed on by this stage and it upset him that they couldn't share that moment. Martin went to see a therapist about the soldiers in his head and the nervous looks over his shoulder. He pulled out every memory he could find, took them apart and found out that everything he'd been doing, he'd done for his parents.

Through his work, he wanted to speak up for them; to tell the guns to hold their fire. That's what they had always said and when he thought of it, that was what he was saying from behind his lens.

4 The Stranded Whale

AS ALWAYS, Peter was only trying to help. The school across the road from his house asked him to build the whale for their summer play and Peter couldn't have been happier to oblige. He was quite excited about it to be fair. He spent all day under the small tinned roof of his studio moulding it, crafting its fins from wire and imagining the children's faces. He fell in love with the idea. He put his whole heart into it and let it swallow him up, gulp him down into the blue painted belly of his own artistic world. He was too close and far too deep to see what it was that he'd done wrong.

But that was Peter.

He was always getting ahead of himself and paddling through his own thoughts, seeing things in his own particular way. He was born a shy boy. He grew up in a town called Molestown in the English midlands and it hadn't got an awful lot going for in 1945. It had a main street and a clock, a couple of chapels for the Methodists, the Protestants and a church the Catholics had built themselves. They couldn't have gone on without it. It was at the very, thudding heart of their community and it brought them together over there.

It was just like Ireland.

It was a grand and friendly place for Peter to grow up. His grandfather had walked there from Roscommon for the work in the mines and it was mostly Irish men down there holding the lines in that sooty smog. They had no other choice than to let their faces and their lungs turn black with thick charcoal.

It was a job that paid well.

Peter's father worked there too. But he shouldn't have. He had tuberculosis and it was a death sentence. Peter never got hugs or kisses off his father who was afraid he might pass it on. They got a coal allowance for working in the mines and that kept the children warm and cooked their meals.

A lorry called around to the house looking for him every couple of weeks. It dropped big boulders of coal on the lawn and his father didn't just throw them to the fire. He would cut them down, gather and stack the smaller pieces while Peter watched. His father knew the grain and grate of the coal, how to lay them to light them, to cinder and ignite them and it was an art form really.

Peter's mother swept out the open fire every evening. She was very energetic, always cleaning and polishing. She was a great woman to do the shopping. She could haggle her way out of a hole and it embarrassed Peter so much. He had three brothers and a sister his mother had to feed.

His parents were great believers in God. They sent him to a Catholic school with one wooden room and a curtain separating the principal and the blackboard. It was quite pathetic looking back on it. Peter behaved well for his parents'sake. They educated their children too with stories they told by the fireside at night of growing up in Ireland.

They talked about their parents, their cottages and how they arrived in Molestown with nothing other than their rags and the Gaelic on their tongues. Always, they would stress how someday they wished they might return home. Peter never understood the yearning his parents had to belong. He was a child and everywhere he looked it was just beautiful. There were trains chugging their way across the heath and sounding their whistles for the people of Molestown. They slowed to a halt and steam billowed from every fluctuating pipe.

They were magnificent!

The scent of hot soot drifted up the street towards his lovely house with its big garden and bay windows where he waited for another one to pull up.

His imagination washed him down and left him wandering about, admiring the flesh and face of nature in its green broad sweep. He visited the reservoir that had been filled with the pumpings of water from the mines and contemplated the enormity of each and every leaf that fluttered to the ground before him.

He spent his childhood summers out on his uncle's farm. There were a couple of horses, chickens and 11 cows, all of which had pet names. Peter milked them and made hay, cut kale. It was a marvellous time for him. It was only a bike ride away and there was something about it, something pleasing in the way the trees wrapped and twined, torso to torso each way he looked.

He was enthralled.

He traced the velvety curves of the brown mountains against the sun and sketched the bushy clots of the bird nests knotted to the fingertips of the bowing branches. He was in secondary school but was always only a bus ride away to his fantasia. He got to see the medieval towns and cathedrals he'd never seen or dreamt of before. He was drawing more and more and the teachers noticed he had a talent behind his pencil and the silence of his desk.

They asked him to do the artwork for the classroom, to colour in maps and design floral prints for the walls. It was practice and a nice way to pass the day. Peter made as much art as he possibly could. There were college scouts that visited the school at the beginning of each term. They selected students to do workshops in different colleges and they invited Peter to spend a day in the art college every week of his final year. He applied to go to college there when he finished school in 1961.

He got in and enjoyed the short year he was there. He wore his college scarf with pride and adored the academic life, the sketch pads and the crest. However, his mind would often stumble upon a priory where he'd gone on retreat with his school. It was a huge three-winged gothic building and they stayed there, prayed there. He sat, quiet and still, sketching the monks in their black and white habits with their rosary beads hanging from their belts. The bells called them to prayer, it was a very romantic way of life and Peter was besotted with the place, its arches and its gardens.

He was 17 and dripping with the enthusiasm of his youth and his wonder. He left college and joined the Dominicans as a lay person. His parents were surprised. It was a very unusual thing to do and it meant they wouldn't get to see him very often while he was there. They were proud of him too. He had his own room and worked on the lawn where a huge gale had knocked down bushes and exotic flowers that left a sweet spice in the scent of rain and wood.

It was sublime.

The lay people took it in turns to get up first and make the coffee in the morning. Peter knocked on all of the doors, gave the blessings of the Lord and looked out the kitchen window and into the morning dew. He saw rabbits and hares bouncing across the face of the dawn.

They read the gospel during the first half of their dinner and a story or a piece of travel writing for the second. Peter could have been eating day old fish and thinking about Italy or J.R.R. Tolkien's, 'Lord of the Rings.' He got his hands on the whole collection and read instead of praying. The pages came to life and the days drew to a close with the halls and the shoulders of their robes lit by candles and moved by the sound out of the Gregorian chant.

Peter met people from all different walks of life. There were war heroes and poets that were writing books and preaching, listening to Joan Baez and prophesying. They were intellectuals. They'd brought all of their problems and their pasts in there with them. They were never what Peter expected them to be. He was the youngest and learning about things he would never have learnt about back home.

He was there for four years and eventually it was the loneliness that got to him. He'd never had a girlfriend before and certainly didn't know how to go about getting one. He realised he was way out of his depth and he couldn't live without falling in love. He left and found it rather unsettling to be home again.

Life was different too.

The mines had closed down and the trains had stopped shunting and spewing towards the children who no longer had the reservoir to swim in and no reason to forget their shoes and chase the clouds of smoke that swallowed up the sky.

Peter was older and at a loose end in his life. He didn't know where to go and ended up working in a factory, stamping tins and packing boxes for a year or two.

He was floundering for a big wave to roll him up off his knees and out of the mundane. He hadn't painted in years because he'd lost the time and the motivation. He missed the pleasure of the stroke and remembered the freedom it gave him to colour his own point of view. He started night classes for the art in the next town. He cycled three times a week straight after work. He got his dinner from two widowed ladies who cooked him his food on those brisk evenings.

They left a stain of kindness on the clean sheet of Peter's years and talked about their journey as sisters from Ireland to England. They never got used to change or the distance between them and home. It just wasn't the same and that shone an unforgettable light on those stories Peter's parents were forever telling.

He was 22 and eager to drench and drown his sorrow in the fountain of his epiphany. He bought a plane ticket to Dublin. His older brother had been there a number of times and organised for a friend to meet Peter and his younger brother when they arrived at the airport. There was a young woman waiting for them with Peter's name written on a sign and smiling.

That was Rose.

She was absolutely lovely and very funny. She showed them around the town, walked them down the streets of their parents old worlds and took them dancing out in Howth.

It was incredible.

Peter felt at home on those cold cobbles, in the wool of the grey day and under those charmingly soggy roofs drinking tea. It was everything he ever imagined and it wasn't long until he had to go home, back to labelling tins and trying to fit in.

It was a cold, cold winter and with it came the snow and the dark evenings that left Peter feeling foul. He arrived home late from class one night. Rose was sitting by his father's fire. She looked astonishing in her cloak; Peter would have been there earlier if he knew she was coming. He would have dropped the ball of the earth to have the evening with her. They had kept up a relationship through letters and he had invited her to come visit if she was ever in England. She came but she couldn't stay. She had to catch the ferry the very next day. When she had gone, her scent lingered in Peter's mind – he wrote to tell her he loved her.

Why she didn't drop him like a hot-brick, he didn't know.

They'd never even been on a date or alone in one another's company. But he loved her. He was writing two letters a week to her and she always wrote back. She was five years older and she had no problem in telling him about her life, the repressive regime of nuns and the catholic school, the rosary and the drive up to Dublin to become a nurse.

He had a picture of Rose and her dark lashes and her heavy lips kept safe in his wallet. He had to be near her and he saved enough money to get out of England and rent a small apartment in Dublin. He could follow the thread his parents had been pulling and telling him about ever since he was a young boy. He was going home. Ireland was the only place in the world that had what Peter was looking for and Rose was there waiting for him at the airport.

She was exquisite.

He even remembered what she was wearing, the brooch she had pinned on and their first kiss. He was so lucky, so blessed. He gave her all of his time and affection, took her to the park and for dinner and drew her little pictures of the big future they had. Peter was always a bit of a romantic and Rose was very practical but she liked the images he conjured up for her.

They were married in 1969. They bought a house and danced circles around the kitchen. They had three children together. They watched them tumble, paint and race the low flying birds around their back garden. They had rows like everyone else. They hurt each other and saw the world in very different shades.

They were an unlikely pair but they were useless apart.

They were a team.

Rose left work after they married. She raised the children and Peter passed all of the exams he needed to qualify as a secondary school art teacher. He got a job up the road from their house and it couldn't have been more perfect. He was there for 29 years. When he retired he built the studio that cramped up their garden and was forever doing things like agreeing to papier mache the whale for the school play.

He had landscapes and canvasses stacked and piled on top of shelves that he'd carved from his own wood down there where he spent most of his time.

Rose hated it.

The place was an organised mess and there was no room for anyone else, never mind the pot-bellied creation he had hanging from the ceiling to dry. He hadn't changed a single bit and Rose hadn't stopped pottering around the kitchen, opening and closing cupboards, coming and going all day long with her perfumed neck and her silver hair.

She forgot what they were having for dinner and made her way down the garden path. She didn't know what Peter had been thinking. He was chuckling from the other side of the whale. Rose shook her head like she'd done a million times before.

That was Peter.

He'd always let his heart get the better of him just like the whale. It was too big. He wouldn't get it out the door for the school. Rose knew she would have to break into his thoughts with this little bit of pragmatism, for it was her face that would draw him back out to the surface of his imagination.

The whale was them, you see.

She told him it was a bit big to take out of the studio. He frowned at the realisation but smiled when she assured him that after dinner, they would work out a way to get around the problem.

That was Peter and Rose. Useless apart but together they always found a way.

5 Call Of The Island

TIME DOES not exist out there on the island. There was no orchestra of clocks ticking, no hour that governed the people's lives. They were free to survive there. There was no law.

There was the people and their pride, their joy in the silent surrender of their days. They didn't want for anything. They had the tide inhaling and exhaling its wet breath as it washed the dirty pearls of the rocks and the hard neck of the cliffs all day every day.

Thomas loved that island.

How could anyone not?

It never changed.

It was the people who came and went, with entrances and exits from their plots of crops, their animals and their dwellings and gardens. They'd built walls with stones they pulled from the ground for generations to make better fields and fences. They'd thatched their cottages, their school and their pub from the reclaimed land.

They were never idle.

They had their own way of doing things. The women knitted the clothes and did the homework with the children, milked the cow and carried the washing up and down to the well where they sat and talked about the weather.

The men were farmers and fishermen. They spent their days out on the rocks or in the currachs. It was their lifeline, their only way in or off the island for their turf. Thomas's father threw him out and into one as soon as he could walk. His father taught him how to bait fish and rotate the oars through the black marble of the night.

Thomas liked exploring.

His parents would send him out looking for dry seaweed or dried cow dung to light the fire and Thomas would get lost over the hill and in the forts of collapsed stone and moss. He never had the chance to be bored. He had his imagination. He would take over the island with the stick of his sword and the howl and the burl of the sideward wind would try and stop him.

But he would conquer it.

It was his nursery.

He was eight years old in 1947. His parents grew up a stone's throw apart from each other. They had 10 children and not a lot to go around. They lived in a whitewashed cottage with three rooms and a kitchen where they did everything by the fire. They had stools they carved from the wood they found and a cow, a donkey and a few sheep in the garden.

They were like everybody else.

They went to mass every Sunday. They priest arrived on the beach in his boat and rang the church bell, filled the aisles with every person on the island. They followed his rules, went to confession once a month and let him sleep in their homes for he had no place of his own.

Funnily enough for a man of his era, Thomas never really believed in the cloth or the bible. He liked to make up his own mind. He knew enough about himself and nature not to appreciate the belts in the mouth and the Hail Marys he had to say when the priest called around to examine the children in his school.

Thomas never liked going to class. He didn't like being confined to the four walls and the whip. It didn't make any sense. He could see his parents outside in the lovely weather, working and enjoying themselves. He knew it was the work that would teach him and at 15 he was ready to begin his apprenticeship through life.

He left school.

He heard that the world was an awful big place and he wanted to get to out there and learn something for himself. He joined the army with his older brother; he needed permission from his parents to go. They didn't complain. It was Christmas time and the currach rode slowly with the cadence of the sea. The island was sleeping. Thomas felt his heart pang as took one last look at the island, trusting it would always be there, waiting.

He knew he would always be welcome there.

He was stationed right across the water in Galway. He got clothed, fed and paid for getting up at seven o'clock in the morning and pinning the corners of his bed nice and tightly. There was no fooling around in there.

The generals were strict and mindful of their clocks. Thomas' time was not his own, that was the first thing he learnt in the four months of his training. They gave him a gun to shoot and practise with on the range and then sent him up the north to be a prison guard.

The cells were full of IRA men singing in a solemn tone and beating their ballads off the walls. Thomas couldn't talk to them. He wasn't allowed. He had to stand in one of the four towers surrounded by spiralling wire and steel bars, overlooking the jail. He held the long, cool neck of his rifle hard against his chest. He was used to it by then. He'd met a couple of characters in uniform who taught him how to speak English, patrol and place bets at the Galway races.

He was doing well.

He was enjoying himself and saving his money. It made the world go round, he was told. He would need it. He moved over to Wales with his brother for the company, the work and the adventure.

He liked it there.

There were waterfalls and a quietness he recognised in the mountains. There was a pipeline building its way through the forests and Thomas was fastening up its bolts, working seven days a week. The money was good because it was a dangerous job.

But he took the risk.

He had a bed and whatever food he got in the lodge had to do him. The people didn't have much themselves. There were hardly any shops or restaurants around. There was nothing to do other than go for a drink, that was it. He was there 11 months. The wilderness gave him a real itch for the throb of a city that's always open for business – London.

There were big red buses revving their engines behind every corner. There were cars beep-beeping and pigeons flapping and twirling into the air and chasing the breadcrumbs children threw up in the air for them. There were crowds of men and women everywhere. Oh Mary, this London's a wonderful sight alright!

There was noise.

Thomas wasn't used to so loud a life. He was pushed and pulled through the herds hustling and bustling across and down the thick streets and on the tube.

It was crazy.

He loved it.

He went out more and more, dancing, drinking, flirting and stumbling home the next day to start again. There was too much to do and see there. There were a lot of Irish people that had never done anything for themselves and their families thought they were well off living in London.

They were wrong.

Those people had nothing. They would drink themselves under the table and save up some money to go home, get scared, buy another bottle and roll over into another drunken stupor. They were too ashamed to go home they told Thomas. He felt terribly sad for them. He wrote the odd letter to his parents and sometimes they wrote back.

Thomas was in London for three years when he noticed the days had begun to trip over themselves into nothing new. It was time to get out. He had a sister living in America and he could stay with her for as long as he liked.

It took him months to get a job in the US- he found the people hard to understand. He made a mistake going there. He didn't settle until he got working and saving his money to buy a car. Once he drove 850 miles towards Chicago where there were police with their batons and their gas, protesters and students with their peace and their bludgeoned crowns.

The Vietnam War was going on and the nasty politics of race devoured the streets. Nowhere was safe. There were poets calling the government's bluff and soldiers who were not looked upon as heroes coming back from war. They smoked pot to forget rather than celebrate.

Thomas smoked it too.

He enjoyed it.

It was their culture, their way of doing things. He understood that and learnt a whole lot while he was there. He picked up a bit about refrigeration and welding and made enough money to make a good life. He rented a house with a small garden and made a home for himself.

❈   ❈   ❈

He met his wife, Molly, while he was there. She was the bartender in the pub across the road from his house. She had short brown hair, curves in all the right places and Irish grandparents. She told Thomas all about them. He saw her almost every day for two years. He never thought he stood a chance with her until she asked him one night if he was ever going to buy her dinner?

Tomorrow?

Tonight?

He would have brought her anywhere, anytime. She told him, Tuesday would be fine.

They had the same sense of humour and pride. They understood each other and the way they liked things done. They were happy together. Thomas would wait for Molly to finish her shift and walk home with her, open doors for her and marry her if she would let him.

She would.

They were married in a Catholic church and Thomas sent the photographs home to his parents who wrote back telling him they would like to see him and meet Molly.

She was pregnant by then and there was no way Thomas could go at that time. They had a baby girl.

And then it hit him for the first time in years. The sense of belonging, of family and where his roots were.

He missed the island.

He'd been gone a long time. He'd seen his fair share of the rest of the world and his daughter was plenty excitement and wonder for his tired eyes. He wanted to go back to where the wind would cradle her down the old dirt roads of his youth and keep her warm. She could play with sticks and pirate her own ship made of stone.

Molly liked the idea. But they couldn't leave. They had too much to do where they were. She didn't have the time to think about it until Thomas' mother died.

He went home.

His father and his brother met him on the coast of Galway in the currach. They sailed against the slight rock of the waves and spoke about the years, the lives that had passed. Thomas's mother had never changed, his father said, nothing had. Thomas could see the white beard of the sea lapping up the sandy chin of the island on the horizon.

It was the same.

He smiled and let go of the breath he'd been holding since Boston and drew in every nuance riding on the salty air. It was terrific. The people remembered Thomas and told him they were sorry for his loss. He'd missed the funeral and stood by his mother's grave for hours talking, telling her about his life, his adventures and his family.

They said she was very proud of him.

His father told him about the pub that was for sale on the island. Thomas rang Molly that day to tell her. He was mad, she said. They had too many responsibilities and reasons not to go. Thomas couldn't think of any. The pub was going cheap. They could afford it with their savings and live on its profit while they were waiting to sell their house.

They had nothing to worry about.

It would be just like he said.

He promised.

He missed his flight back to Boston and she wasn't annoyed. She was nervous though with her own decision to fly over to Ireland two months later. She couldn't believe it. Thomas had sent her photographs of the island and they were tall tales compared to what her eyes beheld. Their daughter clapped her hands for the entire journey in the currach.

Molly and Thomas held each other right through the journey. He hadn't ever been happier.

They bought the pub and lived in it and slept on chairs for the first couple of months. It was rough. The pub was the social place on the island and the people were drinking more and more. It wasn't too quiet in those days. The people were up there every night. They had guitars and Irish dancers flicking heels to toes like machine gun fire.

Thomas didn't do too much on the land.

He was too busy.

He was watching his daughter grow up and disappear through the fields and over the walls discovering the paths he had traversed towards the very same school. Molly wasn't doing as well. She was struggling with the language, the distance the island put between her and the tumult of the town. She was checking the time on her watch all too often. She was making up excuses to row back to Galway and she was moving there, she told Thomas.

She'd tried her best.

She was out there sitting on the walls, talking about the wind, the lack of hail and she couldn't do it anymore. She couldn't live there. There was nothing for her to do and nowhere for her to go. She'd done her best for Thomas and he could only do the same. He went with her to Galway. It wasn't too far away. He could go back to the island any day.

He would be fine.

He promised.

They sold the pub and got a house in an estate with a garden and a swing his daughter was too old for. She changed school and made new friends, kept up the Irish she spoke so fluently. Molly got a job in a hotel and joined the local women's clubs and societies. She settled in and never looked back. Thomas was doing bits and pieces here and there. He was drinking in different bars and chopping wood in the garden. He was trying to make it work, trying to fit himself into some nook or unsuspecting pocket of a stranger.

He liked Galway.

But it wasn't the same.

The streets were alive with racing fever with the passing feet on the paths. They were all in a hurry and Thomas couldn't keep up with them or the years. He was taking the ferry back to the island more nights than he was eating his dinner at the table with Molly.

He was lying to her and to himself.

Molly had a whole group of friends and a network of hobbies and events in Galway. Thomas had a monthly ticket to the island, sore feet from the travel and a yearning in the pit of his gut telling him to go. They were too old to be getting in each other's way. There was no one to blame. They loved each other and they'd both done all they could. There was no helping the fact that they wanted different things. He had to move back to the island, he told Molly.

He was sorry.

She let him go.

They were still married and talking on the phone all of the time. They were making plans to visit each other and their daughter, their grandchildren. There was nothing sad about it. Thomas was very comfortable. There was a fire whispering in the corner and a pile of logs waiting to be thrown in on top of it. He'd cut them up himself. He knew it wasn't easy living there and time would eventually win out and bury him with his parents.

He didn't mind that thought in the least.

In fact, he embraced it.

6 The Porcelain Doll

THE COMMUNISTS took Albania in 1945. they gave the Albanian people their rations and their rules, their regimes and their offices for their strife. They ground them down. They took away their chances for a better life. The people had no choice. They had to work for the government that was chewing them up and spitting them out. They couldn't fight any more. They'd seen war after war, Mussolini and the Nazis leaving them a jangle in the old man's pocket of time.

The cities were dead.

The streets whistled with the sound of nothing but sand circling by the corners of parched stone buildings rusting in the sun. Mosques and mosaics crumbled to dust. There was nothing there for them any more. They were slaves. They were broken by the rustic turbine of the day. Their unrest filled the womb of the rebellion. The cities were no place for a child.

xWhen Zhelia was five years old she lived with her parents in a modest house in the city. Her father ran a small shop. Her mother put food on trays in a canteen. They had little time to give her hugs or hope. They felt it would be better to send her away to live with her grandparents and her uncle in the North Albanian Mountains.

Life was better there and safer.

Her uncle was a policeman. He brought her to see her parents every couple of weeks. Zhelia arrived with tears and apples she had picked for them in the forest. Her father gave her a dolly to take with her to mind her while she was away from them, he said. Zhelia loved her little Babooshka and her brown eyes, her pale porcelain skin and her smile that would dimple for eternity. She would tuck her in tight to her chest and lull her by telling her over and over 'I love you.'

She was Zhelia's dearest friend. She brought her everywhere with her. In many ways they were quite alike. Zhelia had blonde curls and an emptiness rattling about her bones.

She lived with 24 aunts and uncles on a farm where they grew and slaughtered their own pigs. They worked hard. Zhelia's grandfather was the man of the house and he was strict. Her grandmother was the one who cooked all the meals.

She went to prison when she was a young girl. Her older brother had tried to flee the country and the government had thrown all of her family in jail as punishment. Her younger brother died there. Gran was the one to tell Zhelia that it was a mean, mean world out there and she would have to leave her dolly behind and grow up.

She told her there was no place for such delicate little things. There was no time for cracking conkers, scraping snow angels or forgetting the cows at the gate and picking fruits until the sun died into the night. There would only be a darkness that had been saturated in fear. Zhelia would have to be brave. She would have to look it in its beady eye and go to school.

She was seven years old when she started. Education was her only chance to do something useful in life. She had to study hard and attend the gloomy cupboard of her classroom everyday on her own. She would run to and from school so fast that it felt like the wind blew soft tornados in her ears and filled her up.

Zhelia missed her dolly and the cold, hard touch of her cheek to her cheek. She missed her parents too, hugging them and kissing them. Her heart leaked without them. She would dart up the creaking stairs after she'd done her homework, open the door to her room where there were clouds and rabbits, horses and blue skies painted to the walls and a tree outside her window. Her dolly stood beside it. Zhelia would kiss her goodnight and climbing into the bare arms of the branches, she would imagine the lights of cities and wait for her parents to come home.

It was then 1990 and a beast was born pitiless and mute. It slung itself from the cavity of the people's plight. They fed it with their anger and let it slurp the spoilt milk from the blackening nipples of the cities and their misery. The students set it loose. They protested and canvassed the streets with their stance. They had enough.

The communists fell.

The people cried, thank you God and Allah but went home to find nothing had changed.

The democrats took over. They gave the people some land.

But they still had no rights.

No justice.

The beast retreated to the sulking sewers, to the back of their minds and kept quiet.

Zhelia's parents came home to the mountains. She was so excited, so happy. She ran down to greet them. She kissed their feet in the traditional way. They spent the night as a family.

Her parents had to get up early and go to work that was all life ever had for them. Her mother worked on the farm most of the time. She also sewed inside at night-time. She was quiet.

Her father was different. He drove a lorry all over the country for months on end, just so he could feed the family. Whenever he came home, he would lift Zhelia up. She felt more of a bond with him and as time went by she would ask him questions like why had he never had any more children? And he would answer. He would tell her he couldn't afford anymore and that his heart was full with her so where would he put anyone else?

The beast was breeding rebels and swines in the cities. There was no telling what was to come in the early nineties. Zhelia was 15. The feelings of childhood and wonder had left her as she studied more and more. She also worked on the farm and when she got a chance she would rest in her favourite tree. There she would dream of the great life that lay sparkling below the patience of the beast.

She wanted better.

She finished school that year. She got a diploma and it opened a door for her. But she was living in the mountains and her family said no to further education.

Zhelia disagreed with them and said she had to follow what she had strived for. She would be careful, she told them. Her father drove her the four and a half hours to the dormitory where she would study to be a teacher for the following four years.

She had no room to bring her dolly with all of her books and as it turned out her father could only visit every few months. It was hard. The other girls sneaked out at night but even so were getting better grades because they came from different cities with better schools. It wasn't fair. Zhelia went from books to bed where she cried until it was time to go back to the mountains. She stuck with it though for those long, lonely four years and the last time she went back to the mountains it was as a qualified teacher.

She had her degree but no job and without one she couldn't afford to stay in the city. She tried but in the end her father came to rescue her. It was a time of transition as all of the people had gone back to the cities with their lives. The mountains were deserted once again but Zhelia's dolly was still there waiting, leaning against the unopened window of her room and her youth.

This time, they felt like they were strangers.

Zhelia, with her brown hair and sallow skin was no relation, no likeness to the self she'd left behind. There was a deadness seizing the arteries of the meadows where she grew up and what she once loved, she now begrudged. She worked on the farm. She sewed inside the house. She secretly counted the time she was missing in the cities that were alive with violence and sirens.

Meanwhile the beast had crawled out from the lair of their trodden lives with a hoarse rasping from the rebels' mouths. It was the people's oppression that had flooded the veins of its beating heart and there was no hushing the snarling rebels that had torn up the streets.

The rebels kidnapped and killed state officers. They were taking the country piece by bloody piece. It was in a state of emergency. The democrats were out and the socialists filled their seats. But there was no law. There were leather-faced fiends with bloodshot eyes and spoons beating against the pots, pans, steel and chests of the people on their balconies and in their flats. It was the only way of telling who was still alive. They were afraid to walk the streets because of the rape and terror. They clutched red poppies by little wooden crosses.

Acres of them.

Oh God.

It was real.

Zhelia had seen it with her own eyes. Her parents were building a house in the city during this terrifying time. The loneliness of those mountains had scared her more than the rebels that were selling women and children and shooting whoever got in their evil paths. She wouldn't stay. She went with her parents and they drove towards the scorching skies together.

They were too late.

Zhelia had missed her chance in the city. Instead of teaching, all she got was a couple of hours work in a coffee shop.

❀ ❀ ❀

By this stage, all of the girls she knew were engaged or married. This was uncomfortable territory for Zhelia, made worse when her aunt told her she had a nice man for her to meet.

Edon. He was quiet, tall and 10 years older than Zhelia. Soon it emerged that Zhelia and Edon was an awkward arrangement. Neither of them had said a single word for days and Edon had already been married. He never said where she had gone, whether she was dead or kidnapped. He only said that he didn't want to talk about his life. It had been hard.

Zhelia stopped asking and in spite of herself grew to like him over the weeks. Like was enough for her. It was her parents though who were unhappy.

They wanted her to find someone better, someone younger and besides they reminded her that Albanian women can only be with the one man.

Zhelia had made her choice. She went to live with Edon after six months. It was only then he told her he had two children, Alex and Alek. They were three and four years old. They didn't know about Zheila and barely knew Edon. They'd been living with their grandparents as he had been working away trying to save money. He was determined to leave Albania with the children. He'd been planning and saving for years to pay $16,000 to get to America.

Zhelia could stay.

She could go.

But go where?

Her parents wouldn't take her and she wouldn't make it back to the mountains without money. She had no choice but to stay; to mind the children and cook their meals, wash their feet and look into the hollow stare she recognised from her own past. They reminded her of her dolly with their little hands, their fragile frowns and silences.

She felt sorry for them.

It was midnight and Edon shook her shoulder, told her to get up because it was time to go. They had to meet the transport van at a secret location. There, another 27 other people crushed in the back. There were no windows. They couldn't see where there were going and they drove for eight hours towards Italy, Greece or Macedonia in a clatter of fear.

Finally they arrived at an abandoned house. They were whisked out and told to be quiet or they'd be killed. They had nothing but a small blanket for warmth during the days they were there. The children were quivering little bundles and Zhelia tried her best to keep them warm. Finally the rebels returned, took them down to a river and directed them into a slowly deflating raft.

Oh God.

They were up and down, up and down, gripping their fingernails for their lives. It was hell. The waves were splashing, eager to eat them and forget them. The transporters would throw them in if they made a sound – they'd never be found. They ordered the people to jump out at the bridge ahead and crawl through the soaking filth to the trees and wait.

A lorry came. They hid in the back, bleeding, sweating, starving. Zhelia was sure they were going to die. She didn't know how they made it. They arrived. But where? There was green, green grass and small stone houses. Zhelia was delirious and was immediately moved to the hospital where the doctors kept saying; "no, no, not America, you are now in Ireland."

They told Zhelia they'd found a coldness in her chest. She had pneumonia. The children and Edon were fine. They had to answer the government's questions. They had so many questions but unlike Albania, there were no guns, no threats, no knives. It was't so bad. They sent Zhelia and her family to live in Mosney. They gave them a room and some food while they waited on an approval to stay.

They settled in.

Zhelia got better, quickly learnt the language and talked to the people. They were funny. They complained about the rain and the quietness of their days. Zhelia loved it. The children were playing with other children and it was laughter that drew the tears from their eyes and filled them up. They had the time they needed to have childhoods. They were precious. They trusted Zhelia. They called her mother for the first time.

Zhelia cried with joy and she grew with her new family to enjoy life in Ireland. Her family got permission to stay and they rented a house. The children started school and Edon and Zhelia bought rings. They had jobs.

They were happy.

They heard the beast had been hanged in Albania. The people were making their way back to the mountains. Zhelia thought of her parents who she hadn't spoken to in years. She missed them dearly. She had to go back. She found out that her uncle had been shot and buried. She needed to see the grave.

Her parents were so happy to see her. They kissed her feet.

They asked about her life, said a prayer for her family and told her the route through the forest to the foot of uncle's wooden cross.

She fell to her knees and said goodbye one last time. She let the wind gather her up.

Back at the house, her mind oscillated between the old and the new and as she climbed up the stairs to her old room. Zhelia brushed away the silver stitching of her absence and there beneath the spider's prey, her dolly stood faithful and waiting by the window. The twists and tyranny of fate had cracked her face. But she was still smiling after all those years.

Zhelia looked out the window and into the birth of a different darkness.

She took her dolly with her.

This time for a better life.

7 The Ice Cream Van

IT WAS no word of a lie. Christy never had any luck. He pulled a pot of Christmas pudding down on top of himself when he was two years old. He shrivelled up in the corner with his eyes melting shut. The ambulance took him away and he spent the rest of his childhood in and out of hospital.

There was nothing to do. The place was outside the city and they kept all the children that weren't wanted out there. They were disabled and they couldn't speak. Christy couldn't make friends or walk after burning all of the skin off himself.

He shined the floors.

Honestly.

The nurses and the nuns tied a blanket to his butt and his chest and he slid himself up and down, under the beds and around the corners. He was glad to do it. It took his mind off his family. The hospital was too far out for them to visit and he missed them. He was five years old and the doctors told him he could go home. He was full of life and bouncing around his parents feet. He couldn't have been happier to be there.

The doctors strapped a steel frame around his legs and hung a rubber tire from the bottom of his boot to keep him steady. His parents had him out selling newspapers and collecting coal looking like that. He picked the cigarette butts off the ground for his father and trimmed them with a scissors, put them in a jar and if he got a bit of black in it, his father would tie him to the bed and whip him.

Those weren't the good days.

He was out hobbling and playing on the cobbles with the lads when there was a meeting in the corner. There were two girls going to the toilet behind a wall and the lads were all saying that they could see them.

The lads hoofed Christy up to have a look and the girls turned around and caught them. They all fell down and took Christy with them. He blacked out and woke up in the same withered ward he was in before. He was still shining the floors and he didn't know how many times they operated on his leg.

They couldn't get it right. They told him he was going home when he was nine. He just needed one more operation and he would be fine. He was delighted. His mother came to get him and asked him why he wasn't dressed or ready to go home. He told her they did the surgery on his good leg and his mother went down to get the doctor to find out the story and walked back up to Christy with some chocolate and a packet of Tayto in her hand. He knew something had to be up. He never got those kinds of things for free and his mother kissed his cheek and went home with the surgeon's £20 note in her purse. Sorry about operating on the young lad's wrong leg, but sure, he'll be alright in no time.

Talk about bad luck. When he was finally well enough to go home he knew he had to pitch in and help like the rest. He rolled up his sleeves, got stuck in and earned a bit of money for his mother.

She reared 15 children and worked part-time in the bank. She sold GAA tickets on the street and tinsel on the stalls at Christmas. She would be out until all hours and she mightn't make a buck. She wasn't too lucky either. His father used to beat the living crap out of her and she took whatever violence he gave her and got on with it for the children's sake.

She had a heart of gold. She had bleached blonde hair and his father thought everybody fancied her and that she was out chasing the men. Christy couldn't understand it. His mother hadn't a second to spare and his father was an educated man. He was trying to keep her in her place and Christy knew that it was wrong.

His father had a good job down at the docks. He picked the men out for the work and drowned his wages in the pub. Christy was 12 and he was working full-time emptying pockets in the cleaners around the corner. He kept the coins he found and sold the rosary beads the owner didn't want. It kept him ticking over and he was there for six weeks when the bakery across the road told him they would pay him a fiver.

For once he had some luck. He couldn't believe it. He rode a big steel bike with a basket on it. He delivered the cakes and tarts and three weeks into the job, bang. Christy cycled into a guard and got fired the next day. He got a job with a Jewman and delivered leather coats to all the rich that had boats and handkerchiefs tucked deep inside their pitiless pockets. They asked Christy how they looked in their new £500 jackets and he knew what they wanted to hear.

Absolutely stunning, he told them, and they threw him an extra few bob. He had a nice little set up going until the boss came along and made him take eight boxes on the bike. He couldn't see a thing and crash. He hit the pavement and all of the coats were stolen while Christy was stuck under a car.

Sacked.

He went to work for another Jewman making beds. He had a staple gun in his hand and the lad he was working with was bending over. Christy couldn't resist it. He shot him in the backside and the chap leapt the length of the bed and chased Christy downstairs.

Sacked again.

He went to work in a factory and all he had to do was move the bits of timber from one moving belt to another. He tried it. They told him they would lock him in there and kill his parents if he didn't work faster; he was terrified. He found out they were telling lies. He left and went across the road to the matches' factory. The sawdust choked him and the man he worked beside chain-smoked. Christy couldn't breathe.

He lasted two weeks and crossed the road to another factory that promised him more money after a three-day trial. He thought it was a bit of a blessing going in there. But it was a mistake. The men were in the pub at six in the morning and spending their wages going back and forth. Christy went with the flow of the gargle. He was 18 and measuring the days in pints. It was rotten.

His mother's stomach collapsed and she died suddenly. Christy couldn't handle it. He didn't realise how much he loved her until she was gone but he remembered her saying that things wouldn't always be so bad. His luck could pick up and turn around.

Not though when he was a shoplifter and it came all too easy. There were no cameras or bouncers on the doors and Christy was walking in after work and filling his pants with suits and ties and walking out and driving off in cars that had the keys left in them.

He knew it was wrong.

His father died shortly after as if he couldn't live without his partner. Christy then gave all of his wages to his sister – he wouldn't touch her money for a pint. Instead, he broke into Arnotts with two pals and scaled a 40-foot pole, climbed through the barbed wire and hopped across roofs. They were well-oiled to say the least. Christy grabbed a few bob and they drove off in a stolen taxi he knew nothing about.

He crossed his heart. He was sitting in the back seat and they were speeding by the Rotunda Hospital. There was a roadblock waiting for them and Christy was shouting and roaring, gearing himself up for the crash while the car was slowing down. The other lads were holding up their hands, saying sorry and Christy got six months with the lifers and the sex offenders. He repaired the prison walls and stayed out of trouble.

He made parole but got pissed and was 20 minutes late going back to check in two days later. The screws dragged him through the gates and he had to beat the crap out of one them to escape their wrath. He went up to his cell. The others who had gone in before him were there wrecking the place and knocking over TVs, smashing glass.

The screws were killing them. Christy got his bed and put it up against the door. He thought they were going to murder him and he stayed locked in his room for three days. They had to get the priest and the governor to come down and tell him he would be safe. He came out and the guards were standing there in their riot gear. They beat him up, hosed him down and left him naked in solitary confinement.

He went on hunger strike. He wouldn't talk to them or take anything from their hands. He wanted nothing to do with them and they started to worry. They were all over the news and they were trying to be nice to him.

Christy grew a beard and had a think about things. He was 20 years old and all he had was time in there. He realised he never had a dream or any money. His life was a carnival and he could change his luck, he figured. He could try to be a better person and better things would come around.

He made parole again and he was delighted. His brother bought them tickets to go to England for a soccer match. It was supposed to be a celebration. But Christy nearly died. It was the height of the Northern Ireland troubles and when he went through security, the machine went beep, beep, beep. He had nothing on him, but he was brought into a separate room, handcuffed to a radiator and stripped of all of his clothes. They put wet towels over him, beat the hell out of him and left him there with his eyes burnt from their torches. Honest to God, they kept asking him who he was working for and what he was carrying.

He had no idea. He had a steel plate in his leg but nobody had ever mentioned it to him. The English police read it in his records and told him to take their cheque for £7 and get lost. He was in bits. He couldn't wait to get home to fix himself up.

He got his life in order and the boss gave him back his old job in the factory. Christy still gave his sister most of his wages and kept enough for a few cans and tickets to see Thin Lizzy and Led Zeppelin, Eric Clapton and Skid Row in the park. The guards hadn't changed. They found one of their own shot and dead outside the Four Courts. Christy was drinking in town with his mates when a Garda van showed up.

They scattered. Get him. That one. Christy heard them shout and didn't have to look around to know that it was him with his luck. The guards caught him hiding under a truck and took him away, threw him in cell with a blond fella who asked him for a favour. He wanted Christy to tell his family he said goodbye if they didn't see each other in the pub next week.

He was dead.

The guards came back later that evening and pulled the guy out, brought him down to the courtyard where Christy could see them. There was 12 of them standing around him and taking their turns. They spotted Christy in the window and came up to his cell, kicked him out of bed and carried him down to the yard. He knew what was coming and he was going to go for one or two of them while he had the strength. He ran at one and punched him, bit him and chewed the ears off him. The others didn't know what to do and they beat Christy unconscious when they managed to get their hands on him.

They charged him with assault. He didn't say a word in court. He didn't want to make it worse. His auntie kept yelling from the back that the children would starve without him. He was the bread-earner. It worked, he got off with a fine. He was in rag order after the beating. He couldn't get out of bed or make it the pub to meet the blond fella. The guards had thrown away all of his belongings and he had no address to find him. Christy didn't know if he was dead or alive and he thought about him every day.

He cursed his luck.

Christy was the best man at his brother's wedding and he borrowed a suit and picked a fine little thing with curly hair out from of crowd. He had his eyes on her all evening. He was unusually nervous and going up to her, tipping her and running off.

Kathleen was her name and she didn't think much of him. He had big hands and a funny smile. But she danced with him and let him take her out. He gave her timber from work for her mother and he didn't leave her alone.

He kept telling her that he loved her and one day she said it back. He thought his luck had changed after that. Kathleen told him she was pregnant and he asked to her marry him. They were going to elope, but Christy's aunts found out and paid for their small wedding. They had no money and nowhere to go when the bed and breakfast kicked them out the morning after the night of their honeymoon.

They had to squat. They found an empty building with a toilet, a fireplace, a kitchen with nothing in it and when it rained the water came down the chimney and flooded the building. The corporation condemned the building and Christy had to be out by the weekend. A guy across the road told them his mother had died and if they gave him £20, they could to stay in her house. They were sorted and her corpse was in the bed when they got there.

She was smiling. They said three Hail Marys and watched them put the lid on her coffin and carry her out. They weren't there for too long. The guards came and said they'd break the door down. In the end, they had to stay with Kathleen's mother and it was worse than prison. They couldn't leave their room or go to the toilet at night. Kathleen's mother had a screw loose. She stabbed Kathleen under the eye with a fork when she was eight months pregnant. Christy nearly put the ould one through the window. Then Kathleen had told him she was going to change after the birth.

The nurses sent him off to the pub while she delivered and when he came back he was too tipsy to hold the baby but they showed him Sophia, his beautiful daughter. He felt such an ache of luck.

Another slice came when the government introduced a housing scheme that year. Christy and Kathleen could afford a home and there was a bath, a kitchen, two bedrooms and a table, a cooker and then Kevin a year later.

They had no furniture, no worries, good days and bad days. Christy's luck seemed to have improved and then, it all went cold. He took the children swimming in the local pool. He didn't feel too good in the water and the children had to lift him out, carry him home. He made it half way and then collapsed on the street where the people stood around him, judging him and saying, look at him, isn't that terrible? He's locked and those poor children are stuck with him.

Sophia had to run home to get Kathleen who could barely lift him off the ground or get him into bed. He was in a heap and sweating. She called the doctor and he couldn't find anything wrong with Christy. He sent him to the hospital to be on the safe side. They ran tests and found out he had pneumonia.

But it was too late. He died. Seriously. It was so beautiful, so inviting. There wasn't a mark in the sky and Christy was lying in a desert of infallible sand. His parents were pulling him over a hill, towards the yoke of the sun and smiling.

He decided not to go. He wasn't ready. He woke up to the nurse smacking the face off him and Kathleen walking through the door. He counted his blessings and went home to end up back in hospital a few weeks later. He had an abscess in his stomach and the doctors had to cut him open and drain his blood every two hours. He thought he was going to die all over again.

Eventually the doctors told him to go home because they couldn't keep doing it indefinitely.

They were going to remove his bowel and give him a bag instead. Kathleen took him to see an alternative doctor that gave him acupuncture. She told him to go and have some dinner, enjoy himself. He felt better instantly. She put Christy on a strict diet and Kathleen was blending carrots all day and every day for three months.

He didn't need any more operations and he was chuffed. He got back to his old self and got a maintenance job in a college. He was delighted to be working. He was there for 20 years. One day he decided he wasn't going to go in. He booked an appointment with the doctor to get a sick note but with his luck he actually had a heart attack on the way. He busted his nose off the ground and the people stood around, talking and thinking he had a couple of drinks too much on him.

They did nothing. The doctor finally came out, examined him and told him he would be fine in a little while. He should walk up to the hospital and give the letter in his hand to one of the nurses. They did their tests and found nothing. He had to stay the night to be certain. He was giving out about it when he hit the deck again.

They put stents in his heart and sent him home the next day. He still had the bloody tubes in his arms and Kathleen didn't know what to do with him. He was sick. The hospital sent for him two days later.

He had to take it handy, stay at home and rest. But he was dying to get out of the house and when his job finally gave him another chance, he suffered another heart attack.

He was fuming at his luck. In fact, he was tired of it. He had to find new ways to fill his days and he bought himself and Kevin a pair of roller blades. He was flying on the blades one morning. His legs and arms and all were doing it and he was going so fast he couldn't stop.

He bounced off the tarmac and went back to hospital where the doctors told him a blood clot had just missed his brain. He was very lucky that time. But he didn't feel it. He lost all confidence and gave up thinking things were going to change.

Still he went back to school and learnt how to read. He put his head down and came out top of his class. It surprised him. He never did well. He was devoting the rest of his time to Kathleen and they were spending hours walking the beach and talking. He got used to the pace and told Kathleen one of his boyhood regrets was that he never tasted an icecream.

He dreamt about them. Then he lived the dream. He made

his own luck and bought a big colourful icecream van. It was something he always been wanted to do. He was running around like a child when he got it. He fixed it up and took it down to his old area. Kathleen went with him and fell around in the back when he went around the corners. The children would hear him playing the Match Of The Day tune and their eyes would light up the afternoon.

They get the same thing every week. They have a think about their order and he lets them. He gives them his time and sees himself in the sad looks that escape them once in a while. They mightn't have the price of the sprinkles or the sauce and it would break his heart. He would tell them not to worry about it. He wasn't mean like the rest of them. He doesn't count his pennies. He believes there are people who make money and they'll always have some.

He's just not one of them.

He's the icecream man.

The lucky one.

8 Bottles Full Of Empty

BRIDE LIKED the look of herself. She was tall with a thin waist and a big enough bust. She got a lot of attention from the fellas and more than a bit of pleasure out of dancing with them and teasing them.

She was in a hurry to grow up and loved going to the hops in the city five nights a week. She was dancing, cycling and having the time of her life in the early sixties.

She had no great regard for Seanie when she met him. She was 20 and she felt him watching her and taking in the length of her legs from the other side of the room. He was handsome, wearing a leather jacket, skintight jeans and a Teddy Boy quiff in his jet black hair.

He asked Bride to dance or go to the pictures with him sometime and she told him she would meet him next Friday. But she stood him up. She went off and had a ball with her friends and Seanie went to work in England two weeks later.

Bride was happy where she was. She lived with her mother in a small cottage they owned on the outskirts of the city. Her mother had her spoiled. Her father died from meningitis when she was seven months old. She had a photograph of him somewhere and her friends, Nora, Peggy and Maura to keep her company.

Bride's mother minded them when their parents went to the pub. Her mother didn't drink that often and Bride didn't think she would either. She tried it when she was 14. She was working in a factory with the girls and they bought a big bottle of cider between them. They wanted to have a taste and they were all locked and laughing. They swore they would never do it again and that was the end of the drinking.

Bride had bigger things on her mind. She fancied herself a singer. She used to walk two miles to the restaurant closest to her house and stick her forehead to the glass window, look in and think, it was well for some. The men and the women were in their suits and their gowns. They were toasting their fortune and there was a lady standing on stage and serenading them with her swaying hips.

Bride wanted to do that. She practised in her mother's mirror with her wooden hairbrush and sang while she walked, washed and did her make up. She never gave it up. She entered competitions and came second in the Rose of Aranmore. She was doing well and then she never got any further. She tried singing different songs, entering different competitions and wearing different dresses.

Then she got tired of herself. Most of her friends had fiances and they couldn't listen to her or dance with her anymore. She was by herself an awful lot and thinking about Seanie more than she ever believed she would. She wondered what he was doing and what might have been. Out of the blue she heard he was home. She wrote him a letter saying 'sorry' for what she'd done on him and asked him to come and meet her, forgive her and give her another chance.

She was scared she was going to be left up on the shelf and even more terrified that Seanie would stand her up and make an idiot out of her. She was wrapping her hair like a noose around her nimble finger and waiting for him. She could hardly breathe with the nerves or the cold of the snow outside her house.

The moon was bright and full as a pearl. He showed up at her door wearing his leather jacket. He hadn't changed. He was quiet and Bride could tell there was something more to him. The more she got to know him, his quietness seduced her, pulled her in tight, held her up on her toes and owned the coy flush of her lips with his strong grip and his flattery. She saw him a couple of times a week. He took her out on his motorbike and it ripped her tights.

They were together a year when he asked her if she would ever think about marrying him and she said she would. There was no real romance to it. They were married and Seanie lived with Bride and her mother. She was pregnant and she had a little boy who everyone simply called Junior. Her hands were full with nappies that needed changing, dinners that weren't going to cook themselves and rocking Junior to sleep.

She sang.

Seanie rolled over, coughed and told her to keep it down, shut the child up. He hadn't worked since he hurt his leg in England and he couldn't stay around the house for more than hour or two to mind them. He had no interest. He was going to the pub and he wasn't listening or saying a word to Bride about anything.

Her mother looked after Junior if Bride had to go the shops or for a walk to clear her head. She warned Bride about Seanie. He had a temper, she said. She saw him give Bride a bit of a shove one day and Bride would want to watch him. He was going to hit her and one day her mother wouldn't be there to stop him.

She had dementia. Bride went into check on her one morning and found her on the edge of her bed with her legs all swollen. She asked Bride to push her back up onto the bed. Bride had just about got her arms around her when she died. Bride screamed the roof raw and pushed Junior in his rattled pram to the next town in her rush to fetch the doctor.

She was asleep on her wet pillow by the time Seanie came home. He was too late to hold the quake inside of her and he was sorry the next morning. She told him what happened and he tucked her into his leather for the first time in a long time.

She felt a bit better.

But she had to be out of the house before the clock struck the hour of her mother's death and Seanie took her and Junior out to the zoo or to his aunts. He was good to her for those few months. He tried to talk to her and he came running up from the pub one evening. He'd tried something she might like and it might give her a break, he said. It was a great new drink.

Junior would be fine for the few minutes, he assured her.

They would only leave him on his own for 20 minutes and Seanie was right. Bride tasted the tall short and coke he put in front of her and liked it. The white rum filled her chest with a warmth she hadn't felt in months and opened her up. She didn't think she would try it again. She didn't feel right about leaving Junior standing like that and Seanie stopped caring.

He was getting himself into an awful mess in the pub and lashing into the bottles he hid in the presses and sipped to sleep when at home. Bride was left to look after Junior and she played cards with him or took him to the shop. She got a job in the pub after he made his communion. Seanie reverted to type, took her wages and drank them on the other side of the bar. He made an awful eejit out of her and himself and she couldn't listen to anymore of his yap, yap, yapping.

He always wanted something.

She pretended to be asleep so that she couldn't hear the tip of his wet breath by the bed or wrapping the slimy spindles of his fingers around her purse or her throat. He wasn't quiet in those days. He didn't think twice about hitting her a dig, just as her mother had forewarned. He had her battered, bleeding and scraping the shards of herself off her mother's carpet.

For all that he had love in him but couldn't show it.

He was down in the pub telling all the other people how great his son was and then coming home to kick him, whip him and break the skeleton of him. She had him spoilt! Ruined. Seanie would splutter such vitriol from the stained corners of his mouth and he would reef her away from the poor child if she tried to comfort him or pick him up.

Bride could have killed him.

She gave him every opportunity to leave. She would have been happier without him. It was her house and she wasn't going anywhere. But neither was he. He was having too much of a good time and Bride too was drinking more and more, after work and in the evenings when she got home.

She was guzzling the guts straight out of the bottle to forget his face and he was at the bottom of every drink and at the end of every memory. She would only see him, his diluted, red eyes and cheeks and she couldn't look at herself in the mirror. She was still holding down her job and standing under the hanging plume of light at the bar.

She lost all sight of Junior. Seanie was kicking him out of the house and locking him out. Bride never knew where he was but he was working and standing up for himself. He moved out when he was 14. Imagine that. Bride was glad for him. She was drinking from one morning to the next. Her and Seanie passed like ships in night; they slept in the same bed but never together.

They didn't touch. They avoided each other in the halls of the house but drank together in the mornings. They had no one else and they got along for the sake of their headaches. They said nothing to each other and Bride went to work half shot. She thought she was keeping it together. She was earning more money to pay for another scotch, vodka, whiskey.

Seanie had her demented.

He was sick. He was only holding down a pint or two. He hadn't been himself for weeks. He was looking worse for wear and he wouldn't let Bride take him to the doctors. He didn't want her help. But he needed it. He had liver cancer and only seven months left to live. He was on 34 tablets a day and Bride had to feed them him.

She knew what people would say if she made a mess of it. They would have thought she was trying to do him in. They all knew what he was like. They'd seen the black eyes, the busted veins and Junior left wandering in the rain. They took him in, said nothing and let it all come out in the end. They told her she had a problem and she left her job.

She stopped drinking.

She took care of Seanie and bought him the odd drink. She felt nothing for him but the duty in the ring on her finger. He was exhausted trying to hold his head up. He was shivering with life slipping out of him. Bride kept the glass to his mouth. He died without saying thanks and Bride hardly recognised him wrapped in the silk and the wood of his coffin.

He was peaceful.

Death had been kind to him, she thought. She kissed his cold forehead, said good riddance and caught a glimpse of herself in the holy water.

She too was sick looking in her funeral suit. She felt closer to the death of him than the live of herself.

She buried him up the road.

Junior dropped her home after the funeral but didn't go in.

He had to get back to his wife and kids. It suited everyone that way. Bride threw herself at the bottle. She clawed her way down the windowless hall to her bedroom and closed the curtains, to let the liquor loose on her tongue.

She didn't want an audience. Her head was heaving and swimming in the sleepless belligerence she called her only friend. She poured the alcohol into her religiously. She prayed for a bit of rest, a bit of forgetfulness. But it never came. The years couldn't get Seanie out of her head, gaunt and dead. He plagued her with his vulture eyes and she couldn't pluck it from her memory.

She rolled right out of the bed and the gutter of her bedroom floor was harsh on her bones. She couldn't get up. She was old and heavy, crippled with arthritis. The sunlight bludgeoned her eyelids through the curtains. She was afraid to think of how many bottles she'd drunk the night before and all the following nights down to the time it was 15 years to the day that Seanie passed away.

Once again, it unearthed the thirst she'd tried to bury with AA meetings and counselling – something she could never stick with.

She lay on the floor.

She pulled out the bottle of white rum she'd hidden in her bottom drawer and swigged it down to the sweet and bitter end. She sang and Junior found her two days later. She was potent and holding an empty bottle and a hairbrush by her mouth.

She was dead to the world.

She was at peace.

9 The Land Bond

LIAM LOVED the land. He spent his entire life resuscitating it and his roots were knotted in the stalks, whiskers and bristles of the bushes. His family settled there generations ago, out, out as far west as the coast would scroll. It was all bog. Liam was out on it every day in 1961. He was seven years old, helping his father reclaim it with the spades and seeds the cows left behind.

The work was never finished.

He dug his hands into it; he was never afraid of getting them dirty. There were 12 of them in his family and they all had to work. They were living in a small stone cottage overlooking the bay. They had empty teachests from the shop for their cots and his mother split the potato in two to get by. They kept their hands warm above the fire.

Liam's mother cooked their meals over it. She crocheted on her stool in front of it, stirred her jam and churned her butter beside it. Liam's father made shoes for the horses at night in it. Liam marvelled at how his father loosened the iron in the flames.

He showed Liam exactly what to do. He was the only man in the village who killed pigs and his family survived on the bit of meat he got for bleeding it. It wasn't hard. Liam's parents never felt things were hard and they were never worried about it getting any easier.

They could see their crops going further by the year. They were getting back what they put it into the land and it was the best rule to live by, feed their children by, grow old and die by when the time came.

They grew up right across the water from each other. They fell in love and got married in 1946. They were forever standing by the front window of their house and looking out. It was the window of their life, one without money or cars.

There was only one man with a car in the area and he was an old bachelor. Sometimes he gave the children a lift to school and he could fit 15 or 16 of them in it if they put their arms and their legs out the windows.

That made their day.

Liam wished for that old man to show up every morning. He had to walk three miles to school and three miles back. His parents had the farm. It was the only thing that ever made any sense to him and he tried to stay at home as often as he could to help his parents. They got an allowance for Liam going to school and speaking Irish and it was the only reason he stayed on for as long as he did.

In 1969 he left. He couldn't read or write and he went to stay with his sister who was in college in Dublin. He got a job and sent money home. He thought it was the right thing to do because his parents needed money. Yet his mother was sending him two letters a week telling him to come home. He was the only one that had a liking for the land.

He couldn't see past the cranes or their chains and he hadn't a penny or a thing to do in the city. There was nothing free or worth the hassle of his heart and he left six weeks later. He decided it was best and his parents threw a bit of a party when he got home.

He felt right again.

He was slaving into the work and getting more and more responsibility the older he got. He was going to the dances and if they turned him away, he strolled down the field and listened to the band start up with the stars.

On his first real date he took Nora down to the bay. He picked flowers from the sod he'd dug and put them in her hand.

She glowed.

He knew her all his life. His family used to walk across the bay to visit his grandmother and Nora lived beside her. She was always there with her red curls and they played together. Liam asked her to marry him when they were together three years.

She moved in with him and his parents and helped Liam on the farm. He was the only child living at home and grinding out his days on the land. Nora cooked the dinners and gave birth to three sons and two daughters and Liam didn't think there would ever be anything greater than carrying them onto the land and holding them up while they peddled with their rubber wellies in the muck.

His smile grew and grew with sheer happiness.

He never left again.

In 1995, the rain came too late to save his barn from burning down. The flames inhaled the wood, the hay, the tools, the seeds, the crops and the cows that shrieked in shrill agony and cut the tears from Liam's eyes. There was nothing he could do. He had to stand and let it all burn and choke the sky with its spiralling smoke.

There was nothing left.

The fire had stained the earth black where his pride had been. There was a gaping space and he couldn't look at it. He tried working for the council. But he couldn't afford to travel or buy a car and he wasn't able to walk the many miles to the next town in the morning. He went on the dole and stayed in his room for a few weeks. The house wasn't the same.

His mother got ill and passed away by the end of the year. His father then died suddenly too from a heart attack. All Liam had left of their memory was the land. He had to decide whether his family stayed and started again or went somewhere else, somewhere easier.

He knew he couldn't go.

He couldn't abandon his parents buried in the mud and his family's footsteps. He had no choice but to save the land and plant seeds, spread fertilizer and hammer up a new barn. He made sacrifices for his family to survive there. He cut turf and seaweed for years. He fished and his neighbours did what they could to help him. The land was just starting to look right again and then, the priest spoke from the altar.

The poverty was over, he said

Hallelujah!

The men from Combine Gas found gas 46 miles off shore and the priest was the first person Liam heard talking about it. The bishop was on the radio calling it a 'God send' but Liam didn't trust it. The men from the company came and stood on his land in 2000. They were telling him where they were going to dig their trial holes.

They weren't asking him. They were laying a pipe deep into the ground, odourless and experimental. It would lie outside his front door, transport the unprocessed gas from the sea to the plant and Liam didn't get a say in the matter. They told him they had a compulsory acquisition order on his land and Liam told them he needed to see it.

They weren't to come back without it. They sent the gardai to his house the next morning. They told Liam they'd seen the documents and he was to let the suits onto his land to do their work. He didn't agree and besides he hadn't seen the order still. He was trying to protect his home and Combine Gas thought he was stupid, that he would leave and never come back if they paid him the right price.

But there was no price. He wasn't for sale and they didn't get it. He had five different solicitors and none of them got it either. It was easier to take the money. But Liam wanted to give his children the choice to grow up and old there and for his grandchildren to have the chance to do the same. He was embedded in the soil and there was no amount of gold Combine Gas could give him to replace that.

He was out on it every day telling them exactly that and they kept stepping on his land and measuring it. He would kick them out and they would cross into the next field like it was a game of cat and mouse. Liam was tormented with them. They were relentless, telling him they would get what they wanted in the end.

He wised up.

The men from Combine Gas gave each of the people an allotted time for a meeting with them and Liam started going with his neighbours. He knew the men were trying to pull the wool over the people's eyes and get them to sign contracts. They didn't want the people getting together and they built walls to keep them apart after that. There were forms and years of long trips, queues and no answers, no guarantees.

Liam was going nowhere.

They started work on the pipe in 2004. They were going to send him to jail; he knew it. They were going to make an example out of him and he asked for help. But the people didn't believe him. They were thinking he was looking for money and he lost friends over it.

The community was in turmoil.

They didn't wave at each other or meet at the crossroads like they used to. There was no trust left. There were guards knocking on Liam's door. They took him and four other men to court in Dublin. Gas Combine was looking for an injunction and the judge told Liam and the other men that she would take all of their land, their cars and their money if they did not purge their contempt.

She wanted them to say sorry and gave them 10 minutes to think about it. But Liam didn't change his mind, neither did the other men and the judge couldn't draw blood from stones. She sentenced them to jail indefinitely and gave the company their injunction. It led to local journalists crying, families jeering and thousands of people lining the streets to walk in solidarity.

It was all over the news.

It was war.

Liam was never away from his family before and the first two days were bad. He couldn't sleep or eat in the drippy confinement of his cell. He cradled his thoughts and the other prisoners stuck out their heads and asked who he'd robbed or hammered. They didn't believe his story until they watched the news every day and they understood him more and more. They drank cups of tea with him and offered to go on hunger strike for the men. They howled and banged their cell doors to help him through it.

His family was there too. Nora especially. Liam lay awake worrying about her driving all the way to Dublin on her own and she told him not to worry. His sons were looking after the land and Liam was doing the right thing. He had to hang in there. The work had stopped on the pipe and the letters kept filling Liam's cell. They were coming from all over the world. People were writing to him to support him and the politicians were coming to visit him.

He wasn't giving in.

His family was exhausted. They were thrown into the media and Liam wasn't allowed any physical contact with them when they visited him. Their tears fell on the other side of the glass and there would never be any forgiveness for that. Gas Combine left him and the other men in jail for 94 days and they said they could do nothing about it. But then they got too much bad publicity and they lifted the charges on the men.

They were released.

The streets were lined with supporters and the roofs of houses in his village were painted with the words, strength in community and justice. But there was none of that. There were beatings, police baton charges, the pushing and the shoving and the billions and billions of euro the gas was worth to Gas Combine.

There was no end to it.

It was the next few years of Liam's life and he was out every morning. He was there with a few of his neighbours and strangers that had come to help the area. They were stopping and blocking the lorries on the way to the gas plant. They were sitting and shouting at the men from the company to get off his land and there were diggers ordered against them. There were helicopters circling in the sky and dead fish lining the beaches because of the pollution. There were stones getting dug into Liam's ankles while he clung to a truck in protest.

He would have given anything to walk away that second and forget the anger in his arteries. But he couldn't. The alien light of the gas plant was bleeding out from the mountains right across the bay, extinguishing the stars.

He would never leave. He would die first. He was standing by his gate with a marching of blood in his veins and a deafening defiance drumming in his ear.

It was the memories, the silence and the dog coaxing the sheep into the next field, his ancestors and their footprints, his families footprints and his own. They were making him do what he was doing and he had to be patient.

He would wait for the European courts to make a decision on the pipe while the winds from around his land would continue to wail and fill his lungs with gusts of the past. He knew he was right. The land had been fought for once before and it would be fought for once again. He would be there to the end – whenever or whatever that might be.

10 The Bald Dandelion

BERNIE FELT sorry for the poor thing. it was sticking its head out all week. She held back her wish for it to blossom, splatter itself happy amongst the ferns. But the wind stole its chance, its right to grow and blew all of its seeds away in the bat of one good eye. It was a shame really, nobody ever plucked a bald dandelion and she never knew why. She saw a beauty in them and cradled them.

"Bernie!"

Her older sister, Margaret was calling her name and bolting up the garden steps with a cut below her knee and blood crusting. Bernie could see she'd been crying and shoving her tears under her sleeve. Bernie sat her down, took a look at the weeping wound and told her, she was going to be fine.

Bernie would take care of her.

She always did.

She was 11 years old and she minded her seven younger brothers and sisters. She also collected the other children on her road along the way to school. She looked like the pied piper. She didn't mind it. She was good at it and Margaret helped.

They did everything together.

They had to.

Their mother was sick and in and out of hospital with trouble in her kidney. They took it out in the end. She had to be taken care of and the boys were still in their nappies. They needed changing. Bernie and Margaret shared the cooking, the cleaning, the ironing. They were there for their mother.

Bernie wasn't afraid.

Not at all.

She always knew she wanted to be a nurse. Her aunt used to call in every second Sunday for her dinner. She wore her nurse's uniform and talked about her day, the children she saved and the tiny cold hands she held. Bernie was in secondary school and even the nuns knew exactly what she wanted to be. It was all she ever talked about. They knew about her mother too. Bernie and Margaret were in the same class and one of them had to stay home to look after her mother, the boys and the house. The other went to school and got homework. There was nothing else their father could afford to do. He worked Monday through to the dark side of Sunday driving buses and never had any spare money to show for it.

His family had to eat he told the school inspector when he banged on the door. Bernie answered and she didn't know what that man expected her father to say. He was doing his best and Bernie and Margaret couldn't get away with leaving an equation unsolved. Her mother wouldn't allow it and neither would the nuns.

But they understood.

Bernie loved her parents something special. They made time to take the children out on a Sunday morning to the park or the beach. They played with them, talked to them and watched them chasing the shifting sun with their arms around each other.

They were content.

Bernie's mother was getting better and things were going back to normal. Bernie and Margaret went back to school full-time and Margaret left after sitting her Inter Cert in third year. She started working. She never had any interest in going to college like Bernie who stayed and studied hard.

There was a nun in Bernie's school who offered her a summer job in 1972. She thought Bernie would be just right for the work in the orphanage down the country. The nun told her it would be great experience for her if she wanted to be a nurse. She'd never been away on her own before and she spent the entire train journey on the edge of her seat, waiting for her stop to be called.

She didn't know how long it took her to get there. The world had never spun as slow and those tracks had to drop their iron heartbeats to let her off. She'd seldom been more reluctant to move in her entire life.

She'd never seen such a violently beautiful thing. She got off and started walking towards the nun who was waiting for her at the end of the platform.

There was a beakless bird, no, no, a child holding the nun's hand and Bernie was afraid to go near the little boy. He was flapping his arms and bashing his head off the ground. Bernie knew that he didn't want to be there but he couldn't speak. He was exactly how she would have imagined a bird to look without its beak and he was stunning.

His eyes were bold and brilliant and his spine had tucked itself in for flight or from fright. He had spina bifida, hydrocephalus and hair like brown owl feathers tufting at the turn of his incomprehensible neck that had a shunt sticking out of it to drain the fluid. His head was swollen and swinging low. Bernie didn't know what was going on and the nun beside her hadn't stopped talking to tell her.

Yes, dear.

Take his hand.

Bernie did as she was told and ignored him biting and pinching her all the way down to the car. She was terrified. She was 15 and wrote a letter to home the first week she was there.

She told her family they were all off their rockers and she wanted to go home. The wards were chirping and she was too embarrassingly nervous to ask questions or say boo.

She was working from eight in the morning to eight in the evening. She got the children up, washed them, fed them and held up their hands for their jumpers. She couldn't ignore them. She had to talk to them and wipe the soup clean from their chins, play with them as much as she could or as much as they were able.

They all had mental disabilities, physical ones too and nobody came to visit them in evenings. They were nameless, blameless and swept away by a system that left them behind in institutions with their far-off faces and ridiculously wonderful smiles. Bernie grew to care for them and plucked away at each of their problems piece by piece.

She got over her fear and saw the children and their handsome hearts beneath their disfigured silences. She gave them all of her time and affection and they grabbed her, kicked her and stuck by her side like there was no other place for them be. She was there for a month. She tucked them under her skin and came back the next year. She remembered their names and the nurses as well.

They all knew Bernie.

They thanked her for what she did and told the nun in her school how well she got on. The nun wasn't surprised. Bernie was. Nothing had changed back home. Bernie and Margaret were still doing everything together. They went to the discos and watched out for the youngsters under the cabaret of lights.

After sitting her Leaving Cert, Bernie got a job in one of the teaching hospitals for the summer and booked the day off to sit the entrance exam for the Belmessan College that specialised in nursing for the intellectually impaired.

The hall was empty when she arrived – she couldn't believe she got the day wrong. The matron nun came down to show her around and Bernie told her a bit about herself, what she'd done and where she'd been. She never sat the exam. She didn't have to. The nun saw something in her and Bernie started her training in November with the rest of the girls.

She had lectures and full-time work in the wards for the three years she was there. She worked with the children in different environments and she could have gone on to be a general nurse if she wanted to. But she didn't. She was studying to be an intellectual disability nurse and she spent a couple of days in different hospitals and operating theatres on placement.

She hated them.

She was one of the Belmessan nurses and they were considered lower in standing. The ward nurses roared at them and never bothered to learn their names or look at them. They never sat near them in the canteen and the other nurses just went along with them.

They always gave Bernie the case file and the child with the disability. The general nurses would never know what to do and it wasn't that they couldn't, they wouldn't. It had never been a part of their training and Bernie did whatever it took to get through her time with them.

It was always hard.

There were different issues and insults in each place. She had to read the patients files. It was part and parcel of her job and some of them had been in care since 1924. They were locked away in barns or asylums all their lives and it was all because of a lack of oxygen at birth.

She couldn't understand it.

It wasn't right.

There were two year olds left to rock themselves to sleep in a frenzy of tears and frustration. They were helpless and those doctors and nurses seldom tried to look past their lagging limbs, their biting jaw or crooked crowns to find the child beneath them. They stood in front of them with clipboards and frowns, ticking boxes and ignoring the piercing sound of their hungry cries. They summoned Bernie to rescue and she did everything she could to feed those children their dinners.

Her results were hung up on the noticeboard in the hospital. She worked all the time and checked them on her tea-break. She got honours. She was delighted and went for an interview in St. Luke's Hospital. There was a panel of five doctors and nurses who told her she would be working with children who had profound disabilities. She knew how to help them and make a difference. She got the job and started working with the children straight away.

She got to know them day-by-day and very soon they relied on her. She was their educator, their personal assistant, their speech therapist and physiotherapist, their friend and their family. She focused on different ways to teach them and communicate with them.

She convinced the hospital commissioners to rent a bigger room for them in town, where they could play and spread themselves out and where Bernie could lock up their toys, walk them home and take them out into the world, to the shops and hold their hands at the flashing of pedestrian crossings.

She taught them how to cross the road on their own and stir their soup, ride the bus. She had a laugh with them coming and going, balancing themselves on windows and hanging from every word she spoke.

They gave her everything and she reciprocated. The other

nurses thought she was mad sitting in boats they rocked and getting on roller-coasters that made her vomit. She organised parties, sleepovers and trips to the castles, forests, pools and adventure parks for them. She carried picnics to the beach and as soon as they saw the water, they were gone, clothes and all. They needed her assistance and no matter what it was, she did it. Bernie saw what a little attention could do for them; how they could change the very essence of a room or a person and flutter and take off on their on own.

They were special.

There was a boy named Paul in Bernie's unit and he was six years old with ginger hair and green shorts. He had cerebral palsy and his leg muscles were loose as he took his first steps towards her.

The people came from the other rooms to watch him grab a hold of Bernie's hands and they were all screaming and roaring. Those moments were few and almighty in their triumph. Bernie rang Paul's mother and she was never happier.

Bernie was close to the families. They became a part of her life and she a part of theirs. She supported them and told them that every child has the ability to learn and the right to an education. It was something that the old nun from school had told her and it stuck.

They fought for their children's rights because their needs weren't being met. The government didn't care. They were putting the children anywhere and everywhere and the families were tired of it. They paraded the streets and hospitals and brought the government to court when they didn't listen. They spoke up for the children and Bernie worked with the department to develop plans and possibilities for the changeover.

It meant she had to leave the ground floor. She was now fighting on a bigger stage for the same cause, the children who she would never allow this country to forget.

She missed the continuous contact with them. The phone doesn't stop ringing where she works now and it can be too tight for thought sometimes. She takes it off the hook and remembers why she's there, why she never had time to have children of her own or marry and see the world. It was simple really, it was what she was meant to do and she did it.

She grew that bald dandelion a bouquet of yellow petals and gave that beakless bird back his voice.

11 The Ordinary Life

A CRACKLE, a hum and an expectance of warmth. A pair of delicately hands linger above the moist air lifting off the thick black cooking range. It had been heating the oven, hearts, hands and feet beside it for longer than Eileen cared to imagine. But that was beside the point. She lived a very ordinary life and never quite knew what to make of it all; she rummaged through her days and looked around at the world occasionally to question it.

She opened her mind and her eyes too.

She was the eldest of six children, three boys and three girls. They had a privileged life in a way. They were lucky. Her father had a good standard of salary and they always had a car. He took them out on Wednesday evenings and Sunday mornings. He managed the local co-op store for the rest of the week. He was an intelligent man. He taught himself how to write poetry, stories and articles for the Independent.

He left school when he was 15 and got a job in Dublin as a commercial traveller a few years later. He was up and down the country all the time and he met Eileen's mother along the way. She had her own little restaurant in Carlow. They fell in love and got married in 1926. Eileen's father got a promotion up the north and it was like moving to another continent at the time. He got a bonus every year. He bought Eileen's mother a present of a fox fur, a pair of gloves, a watch or a ring.

She deserved it.

She had a woman coming to help her in the mornings. The children did their chores and made their beds. She never walked out the door for a thing. She had the butcher man call round in the morning for her order and drop it back to her in the evening in time for dinner. She had the bread man, the vegetable man, the fish man and the milkman knocking to the door as well.

They rented a great big house with three floors, five bedrooms, two bathrooms and a garden out the back. There was a small scullery where they left the geese, the turkeys and the rabbits hanging. Eileen thought nothing of cleaning out a chicken and plucking it, gutting a rabbit and skinning it.

There were no refrigerators to keep the food fresh. They had salt and a wooden chest with a pierced zinc front on it. Eileen's mother kept it in the coldest part of the garden. She was a clever woman. She kept the children out of her sitting-room. It was the only room that had a square of carpet thrown over it and it was for visitors or Christmas and the odd Sunday evening when the family sat by the fire and listened to Radio Eireann. They were blessed. They had a radio, a three-piece suite and a gracious grand piano, made from black ebony and rosewood in the corner.

Eileen polished it every day.

The children were allowed to practise for half an hour. The candles would be lit and flickering by the ticking of the gold-rimmed metronome. They were blown out when their time was up. The children were sent back to the kitchen, the heart of the home. It had a table and chairs, a hot press and a wooden rack hanging over it to dry their clothes.

They did everything in there.

The children did their homework, played Snakes and Ladders and Ludo. The whole family played cards and ate their meals in there. They told their stories and Eileen's mother did the sewing and the washing before making her jam that summoned every hungry tummy to the range. She prided herself on how many jars of rhubarb, damson and plum she had glittering in the pantry.

The kitchen was average with its lino floors and the range cockling lowly in the centre of the room. Her parents relied on it and Eileen was eight years old when she was warming her hands over it one morning. The bell struck in the fine church across the road from her house and her little palms started sweating.

She'd never seen inside it.

She went to mass back down the hill in the cathedral. The priest dictated their lives from the cradle to the grave and they didn't think for themselves. They never missed a ceremony or an offering. Their status in society depended on how much they paid the priest while he sat ornately by the altar. He made a list of what the people had given him and read it out when they'd finally hushed themselves into an eager silence.

It never aroused anything other than confusion in Eileen. It seemed such a trivial thing. But then, the whole town glossed over its religious politics for money and she couldn't understand it at all. There were Presbyterians, Anglicans, Protestants and Catholics. They all said hello, played golf and tennis and helped each other quietly and privately. They had their own shops and beliefs.

They parted ways for Mass. They wouldn't be caught dead in the other's church or at a funeral. It was business versus religion and that was the way it was.

She watched the people vanish through the wrought-iron gates with their heavy prayer books in front of their lighter faces and wearing immaculate dresses. She was curious about them and the woman who lived next door to Eileen was the church's caretaker. She told Eileen she would bring her into the church that morning.

Eileen met her on the path with her heart thumping. She didn't really think about what she was doing, where she was going. The

Harvest Festival was on and there was something spectacular about the apples, oranges, vegetables and sheafs of wheat that had been laid out.

She'd never seen such a sight.

Eileen's mother had seen her leaving the church and she severely chastised her when she came in the door. How dare she go in there. How dare she. Her mother hissed and Eileen wept. Her father would have high-tea with one of those families once a year. He would tell Eileen they were kind, honest people and that was the strangest thing to her.

Some time later Eileen was walking home in the dusk and she lifted the little moons of her eyes to the sky. It was all shimmering, blues and greens, drapes of light and lace. Illuminating. She never saw anything more enchanting and she cut through the hedges to her house where her father was standing by the window, whispering, Aurora Borealis.

The Northern Lights.

The night WWII began.

A man with no face interrupted the static fizzing over the airwaves. He uttered the words of consequence. War had been declared on Germany. They heard it all on the radio. It was the only thing that really kept them involved. The pictures were silently distant in their black and white and the radio was ringing out with its words like long knives and Lord Haw-Haw, Hitler's mouth piece singing the phrase, Germany calling.

Eileen hardly noticed and carried on her life, her coupons, the rations her father wrapped in little black bags and dealt out to the town. He had to weigh everything out and make sure everyone got the same. It must have given him an awful headache. He had to drive Eileen across the border for a loaf of white bread. She smuggled it back. There were a lot of blind eyes turned in those days. All they had was milk, butter, cabbage and black bread.

There was no sugar. No tea. The war went on for six years. A lot of people left town for the work in the English factories and a lot of Americans hung around, married the girls and took them back across the ocean with them and their chewing gum. There was nothing else that stood out to her.

The men were still going to the pub and the women went to their devotions. Eileen would tell her mother she was going to church and hang around the courtyard down the town instead.

They all did it.

They went to see the lads from the choir and have a flirt over an ice-cream. They called it 'doing a line' if a lad and a lass were seeing each other. They were 'walking out' if it was serious. They strolled around the town for everyone to see that some things never change. There was a barracks at the bottom of the town and Eileen had a friend, Laurel, who was very forward. She had a reputation but she very nice. Eileen thought it was all very innocent the way they went on. Even the travellers over the hill never caused any harm and they had terrible lives.

They came begging to the door, looking for clothes and food. They lived in carts and tents and they didn't commit crimes. Some of them went to school and sat there twiddling their bare toes without ever saying a word.

They were taught through Irish and they had drama, dance, orchestra and elocution. The classes were small and the children were comrades. They stuck together in their stern battle against the nuns who caned them and bound their wrists for using their left-hand. There was no bullying. They all knew they were lucky to have their shoes and their chance to sit the Leaving Certificate.

They published the results of the exams in the newspaper in 1946. Eileen got three honours but she'd never thought about what she wanted to do. She guessed that her dream was to have a house and a family of her own. There weren't very many options at the time. She could have gone to Dublin to become a radiographer if she was clever enough and studied Latin or paid a fee to train as a shop assistant or a hairdresser.

She filled out the extra form her friend had for a home management course in a town nearby and got accepted. The teachers starched their aprons and wore white nurses' hats. The girls did the same. They had to be perfectly turned out every morning. They had to cook, sew, launder and stay in a little flat for a week, manage it and make their own eiderdowns out of silk and by beating the feathers into them with a wooden spoon.

She'll never forget it.

There was a pig's head staring up at her in class one day and she had to dismantle it, take all the meat off of it and boil the skull to make brawn. She used every bit and never batted an eye or complained about cooking hearts or tongues and stuffing them. Eileen was so well-trained she could run a hotel by the time she left there.

She wanted to be a home economics teacher and applied to a college in Dublin, got in and stayed in a hostel with the nuns that fed her plates full of peas and bacon for her supper. The city shook her mind and opened up a wonderful social life. She finished her lectures at four and could go off to the pictures, to the theatre or to the dances.

She could never get it together for the jive. The boys looked one way, the girls looked another and they hobnobbed with each other every evening. There was a ball or a gown to be worn or shared. She didn't miss home. She went there for the summers and not a mind had loosened since she'd been gone. She'd taken out her inner eye and strung it from banners, hung it from words and introduced it to new people.

They made her put it away back there where her father was stern by the range, unchanging through time. Once she brought her father back a book by Frank O'Connor. He only had it a day when he came into the kitchen and dropped the book into the fire.

He didn't say a word but that gesture was enough. It wasn't the same any more in that big empty house. Her father was lonely after her mother had died too young the summer before. She had an enlarged heart and Eileen was upset to lose her, even sorrier to see how quickly the grass grew without her. She realised most of all that she didn't know her parents. They were nice in their own way. They were strict and their children were there to be seen and not heard, kept in line and from temptation. That was all she knew of them.

She got a job in the Gaelteacht teaching home economics and she'd never heard anything like the silence. There was no electricity or streets; there was nothing to do. She found out who had died in the town and went to the wakes for the craic and the banter.

She taught her classes in the kitchen with her old friend, the big black range. She had to cook Christmas dinner for the priest, the teachers and the councillors all the while thinking about the boyfriend she had down in Dublin who wrote her a letter every day.

He also sent her Agatha Christie books to keep her occupied during the working week. Eileen was eager to get back to him and she made up her mind, she was moving back to Dublin. She saw a job advertised in the newspaper and went round canvassing Fianna Fail and Fine Gael for their support.

Her father was furious.

He couldn't believe she was choosing Dublin over her roots. But Eileen had to be selfish. She had to have an inquiry around every possibility and let her eyes settle and roam wherever she saw fit. Her father would come around just like everything else. There was a pattern she spotted and no sooner had Eileen landed in Dublin when her boyfriend had to move to Tipperary.

They hardly met.

It had to end and Eileen was far too busy to worry about it. She was teaching children in three different schools in the mornings and women in the evenings in a different town. They called her the itinerant teacher and she liked it. She was by the coast and its windmills. She went dancing every Sunday night under the pavilion. She noticed a peculiar kind of dashing man across the room.

He was standing in a puddle of milk in 1959. Eileen couldn't take her eyes off him. She knew he was going to be the man she married and she was right. There was something about Phelim and the way he took her hand to hold everywhere they went. He wouldn't let it go in the theatre or at the musicals, the pictures and on a walk in the park where he proposed a couple of months later.

Eileen could hardly remember the ivory of her dress or the small wedding they had. They bought a house outside the city. They had three children and whole new reason to admire the world.

They were happy despite the fact that Eileen couldn't keep her job after she got married. She spent most of her time in the kitchen. She liked to bake her own bread and scones. If the season was right, she would make her own jam and the lava of the bubbling berries would dangle warmly in the air and fill the house. She was stuck with those kinds of traditions and she wouldn't let her children forget them.

When all of the children were in school Eileen began teaching night classes to keep her hand in the business. She was thinking about going back to work during the day. She saw an ad in the newspaper for a class two mornings a week with mentally disabled children. She didn't think she'd be able for it and forgot all about it until a magazine came through the post box a few weeks later.

She didn't know who or where it came from but the very same ad was on the back of it and Eileen answered it and got the job. She was the only person to ring up asking about it and it was a lovely set up. She had to teach the children to look after the school kitchen and to do things like set the table and clean the dishes.

They had a beautiful way of seeing things and they showed Eileen how to focus on the smaller things in their light. She took them to the zoo and the grocery to shop for their lunch all on her own. She got on like a house on fire and she was there for a two years when the nuns started pestering her to teach the sixth years.

They wanted her to go full-time and locked her in the parlour to get their way. She had to sign on the dotted line and look at it from their point of view.

There was a woman who lived next door to Eileen who worked there as a teacher and Eileen drove her to work every morning.

The lady couldn't stop talking and Eileen didn't see the effect she had on her life until she died and Eileen's car was without her cotton perfume. Eileen missed her and her imposition.

Eileen went on to work in that school for 20 years. She witnessed the rise and fall of the universal youth and she had enough of it.

She retired.

❀   ❀   ❀

Her husband got a brain tumour and died very quickly. Eileen hated watching him suffer and she didn't know what to do with herself when he was gone. She joined different clubs, learnt how to paint and play the organ and tried all sorts of things to fill the yawning gaps in her life.

She decided to go back home. She had family left up there and a sister in Africa who was a nun and who invited Eileen to go and stay with her. She didn't need convincing.

There was so much going on out there and she had to take it all in, the thin children with their fat generosity and the men with their guns, their suits and their bulging wallets. She let the images imprint themselves on the back of her eyelids and travelled more, took pictures and wrote things down. Her memories were raindrops tumbling and swallowing other raindrops and it got harder to tell them apart as the years went on. She could count the number of friends she had left or alive on her hands and she was leaving the country for Venice, Rome, Denmark and where ever the wind took her every couple of months.

She took a look at the world again. There was an unusually grey man boarding the same plane as Eileen and he'd caught himself on the armrest halfway down the aisle. She couldn't get by him. There wasn't enough room and she had to help him unravel his bag while trying to fetch her eyes from his curiously aged face. He asked her what she was doing going away like that on her own and if she would let him buy her dinner under the dome of speckled light and life.

Why not, she thought. Life was no great shakes on her own. Besides, she believed that it wasn't the times that changed, it was the people and despite what her parents had engrained in her, she was happy to open up to change.

12 The Butterfly Chase

DEIRDRE WAS born a tiny, hungry handful in the back bedroom of her parents city house in 1955. She had scarcely enough skin on her bones as the neighbours called round asking about the second youngest of 10 children. As she grew up she shared her clothes, her shoes and her bed with her seven sisters. She played house under the stairs and poured salt on raw potatoes and ate them.

They were yummy.

She remembers one day being very hungry when she was eight years old. She had to go hospital suffering from malnutrition and was so bad the doctors kept her in. They put her in a ward full of mothers and the women looked after her and told her she was a heart-breaker with her blonde hair, her lovely smile and the short skip in her step. Her mother hated leaving there. She only had the time to visit her once a week and Deirdre looked adorably frail in her hospital robes.

Her mother devoted every moment she was awake to minding the children and sewing dresses and tablecloths to buy some more potatoes or porridge. That was all she could afford. She had a white handkerchief with a blue butterfly she'd sewn on to it in her pocket. Deirdre knew where it was if she let a tear flop, her mother could wipe it away and tell no one.

Her mother was sitting by a window in Cork and sewing that neat hanky when Deirdre's father first laid his eyes on her. He went back to see her again by cycling all the way from Dublin to walk beside her – it took him three days to get there. He didn't mind. He was in the army, a regimental man. He played music for her mother and when they got married, he got a job as a postman and started drinking in the pub and playing the mandolin, the banjo and the tin-whistle in his room.

He went sour.

He left Deirdre's mother to feed the children; it seemed the only time he went near any of them was to beat them. Her mother was always there to save them when he did.

Away from him, she was a very well-spoken woman and she sat up straight, crossed her legs and put one hand over the other while she watched the children playing in the streets. They climbed up the lamp posts and tied ropes around the tops of them to swing from them and Deirdre couldn't help but get the highest.

She was the smallest in the class when she went back to school after being in hospital; almost inevitably the nuns held her back a year. That meant she was in the same class as her younger sister, Paula, so they shared their books and their stories about the leather strap the nuns wrapped around their knuckles.

But they were fortunate. Their older brothers and sisters were working and the younger ones got to stay on in school because of it. The nuns were always demanding their silence and Deirdre found it extremely hard. She flinched, ran and skid like all the other girls. The boys loved to chase her and she liked to slow down to let them catch her.

Her mother used to tell her to keep the boys wanting and not to be giving everything away. Deirdre knew the game. She got a lot of attention with the coy curl of her pink lips. She went to the ceilis in the sheds where there were fluorescent lights and no dark corners and she was 15 when she got her first kiss, 17 when she moved on to the discos and Sloopys and Charlie's in the city.

She had a French boyfriend, a Spanish boyfriend, a jeweller and a drummer and they were all very interesting for a while. But she wasn't looking for anything serious and she wasn't trying to hurt them. She was following the flutter of the butterflies in her tummy and they were in a tizzy at that time.

One night she was out with two of her sisters who were off dancing with two boys when the last song came on. Deirdre was alone by the side of the dance floor and Niall stole up to her. He nearly knocked her over with the fright. She jumped and the butterflies flapped, tumbled and sprung from the blue hyacinths of her eyes.

Niall looked well.

He was four years older than her and his shoes were polished, his moustache was full and combed down at the edges. He asked her to dance and later paid for the taxi home with her squealing sisters. He had money, they said, hold onto him. He was a builder and he wanted to take her to dinner next Friday.

She began working in an office after she left school in a fury because the nuns pulled her sister's hair too hard one day. Deirdre stood up to them and told them they were wrong and they threw her out. She went and did a typing course after that. Her older sister got her that filing job and Deirdre earned a decent enough wage. She bought herself a new outfit with matching boots for the date. She looked great as she stood by the restaurant and waiting on Niall.

He stood her up.

She couldn't get over it.

She didn't think he was that sort and cried on the bus home. She rubbed her mascara in her sleeve and her mother told her to forget about him. He wasn't worth it. Deirdre went back out with her sister later that night and he was there in the place. He came up to her and swore he was at the restaurant earlier and she wasn't there in time.

She didn't believe him.

They made the same plan for the following week. This time she was a few minutes late and he left again. She wasn't surprised. It was déjà vu. She went back to the club and danced with him again. He'd waited for her for half an hour, he said, they would have better luck next time.

They did.

They went to the pictures and later had a flirt and a kiss in the pub. Niall had a pint and Deirdre had an orange juice and a giggle. She liked Niall's manly manner and he was charmed by the crackle in the cheek that she gave him. He brought it out in her and wooed the flitter of wings that whirled around her chest every time she was near him. She leaned into him and there was nothing she wouldn't do for him.

They'd been talking about getting married and Deirdre was tired of waiting for Niall to do it. His father had told her it was a woman's privilege to propose to a man on a leap year and she did it. She was 23 and nervous as heck on her wedding day. Her mother gave her a tablet to calm her.

The office she'd been working for shut down and she didn't find anything else so they had a small wedding. Niall paid for everything. They used an old pair of rings his grandmother gave them and Deirdre was happy with that. They rented a flat in the city.

She got pregnant almost immediately; Niall was working hard, seven days a week. He came home late when their little baby was born, he would cradle their daughter under the crook of his arm for hours on end.

He told Deirdre about his day and asked how her family was doing. Deirdre didn't have a lot to do and she was glad to have the family to visit. She had no money to do anything else. Herself and Niall were saving up to buy a house and all they could afford was their rent, their dinner and the nappies. Deirdre was oh-so content though as she strolled around the city with a pram that clattered against the cobbles.

Niall found a house overlooking the sea and they calculated that they could manage the mortgage if they watched their money. They would be happier he promised. It was a long way away from the city and it had four bedrooms but no carpets or curtains when they bought it. The walls weren't painted and they had two chairs, a mattress, a cot, a kitchen table and no food or coal a lot of the time. Deirdre was lonely. She knew nobody and Niall was working from seven in the morning until nine at night.

He couldn't take her to see her family or keep her company. She had to find ways to amuse herself and she went for walks on the beaches and twiddled her thumbs while her daughter played. Deirdre counted the minutes until Niall came home and they had dinner and a cuddle and a grin flew across her face again.

With the arrival of their son, she found she had more to do. She settled in, made friends and heard a knock on the door now and then. She liked the place. Niall set up his own business and eventually they had more money. He bought some things for the house and a van for himself with the doors hanging off it. He taught Deirdre how to drive it and she went to visit her family if he wasn't using it. It meant Deirdre would see more of him.

That was all she wanted.

The children started school and made friends of their own but Deirdre still had to do everything by herself. She went to the children's school plays, the parent-teacher meetings and their birthdays by herself. She reared them and Niall earned more money as the years went on but he wasn't really part of the family.

He wanted a bigger house and he bought one further out in the country. That was his contribution.

It had a balcony and carpet, furniture and loads of space for Deirdre to fill. She stirred herself crazy out there. It was even more remote and even lonelier than when she moved before. Nobody knocked on the door and she wouldn't talk to a single person all day. She had to pester herself into caring about their huge garden and folding the clothes that had already been folded. She had another daughter by then and she was thankful for something to distract herself from the gulf of her isolation.

As the business boomed, Niall finally decided to take some time off. He booked their first two-week holiday and Deirdre was excited. She'd never left the country before and Niall could wind down for once and be with them over dinner when she or the children talked to him.

After that he relaxed more and more and caught the golf bug to the point where he was out on the course in the rain, hail or snow. She could hardly get a hold of him. He was gone every Saturday. Then he went drinking with his golf friends when they finished in the evenings. And later they talked about it in the pub. They planned their golf trips to Spain and Portugal and that wasn't the problem. He now had made time but it was for golf, not her and the children.

He was always late and leaving her to sit on her own with his other golf friends and she would be furious. She saw he had lost interest in them. The children would ask her where he was.

She didn't know.

She thought back on their lives together and how he'd been missing for most of it. He always had something better to be getting on with. Meanwhile she was being moved further away from her family and her friends to make him happy. She resented this, she resented him, the golf, the money and the fact that he bought more things, more cars and the house in Spain.

In truth, they were leading separate lives as Niall started going away by himself. Her mother died and Niall was in their house in Spain when it happened. He came back to Ireland as soon as he could. He helped and held her but really she could feel his grip itching to get away from her as soon as they threw the dirt on the coffin.

It wasn't right. She asked him again and again if there was something going on and he denied it. Of course she believed him. She trusted him, loved him and she didn't want to think otherwise. She couldn't bear to.

She was helping him with his post and then she opened up his phone bill. It was over €1000. There was a Spanish number on it and she called it. A foreign girl answered it and Deirdre hung up. When she confronted Niall he reluctantly admitted it. He said it was only going on for three months; she didn't believe him. She grabbed him by the collar, dragged him downstairs and threw him out the door.

Bang.

She called her sisters and hung herself over the kitchen table to cry. It was the worst day of her life and she had to file for divorce straight away to keep the house. She told the children and they were upside down with the devastation, the disbelief. Deirdre couldn't speak for weeks on end. The same questions ran round her head and she didn't know what she'd done wrong.

She wanted to kill him.

When she heard he was home for Christmas she booked a flight to Spain and went to their house. The 34-year-old Russian brunette he was living with was there and she was thin, expensive and swimming in Deirdre's pool, sleeping in her bed. Deirdre told her what she thought of her and threw her out.

She was the millions of tiny pieces of glasses, plates and ornaments she'd smashed off the floor. Niall didn't look at her in court a month later. She swore to the judge that it was what she wanted even though he was the one that wanted out.

She woke up crying every morning because of him. She fell asleep on her soggy pillow and lost weight, hid her wedding ring away from herself and took down the pictures of her family smiling.

They didn't talk for a year and a half. Deirdre rang him to sort out the bills and nothing else. She went away with her sisters and the children had their own lives. Deirdre had wrinkles that were actual miles on her face. She didn't want to burden them.

He called her out of the blue and asked to talk to her to apologise. He came over to the house for hours, clinging to the edge of the seat like an old man that wouldn't let go of his grave and eat the dirt he'd dug up for himself. He told her he hadn't been happy in years. This time she didn't believe him and what's more she didn't care.

She told him she had repayment bills gathering dust and on top of all the other bills the banks were hounding her. She was broke and the halls of her grand house were emptier than the quiet space between her reluctant heartbeats.

She didn't want to see him again. The last two years had gutted her like a mouldy fish left for scraps and seagulls to peck. It was a terrible thing to live with really, the gaping heart, the clean shot, the betrayal. It had taken it out of her and she decided that 2011 was going to be her year. She was going to do what she wanted, when she wanted and her sisters thought it was a great idea.

They took her out to celebrate on New Year's eve. She went outside for a cigarette and when she came back in, there was a big, tall man with silver hair standing by her table, talking to her sisters and asking for her number.

She said of course.

It was time to let go of the butterflies.

13 The Gentleman Beneath

SHIT, PISS, the smell was making Tony sick. There was a mattress swelling and stained in the corner. It was twenty quid's worth of nothing but shuddering walls and he was festering there, rotting away in the sterile scented coffin of the flats. He hadn't showered in weeks and his arms were thin and punctured, crusting with the relief that he had no more.

He was at an end.

He had a rat inside him, nibbling at the meat that was clinging to the ribcage of his mind and it would chew its way to the very heart, if he let it. He had to stop it, kill it or it would kill him and there was a chair propped and waiting beneath the noose. He'd spent the last few days thinking about death and he knew nobody would miss him. He wasn't leaving any broken hearts or open doors behind.

Howling from the sewers of his memory, he wasn't trying to offend anyone. He was never trying to do that. He was only trying to be a gentleman and do just as his mother had taught him back when he was growing up in the sixties. Her words were gentle and hopeful like any mother. She was teaching Tony how to keep his body clean, upstairs and downstairs and like any son, he listened to his mother.

She told him how to address a person and to have good manners by saying please and thank you. He was to respect other people and himself and it would never matter where Tony was from or where he'd been, if he was a gentleman.

It would save him.

She fed the children porridge for their breakfast, tea and

supper when they had nothing else. She borrowed money from the Jew men and they heckled his father if she missed a payment. She had the St. Vincent De Paul call around and give her a bag of coal and a pound or two in a folded envelope.

His father was no help.

He didn't work and he liked clothes, racing-pigeons and the gargle. He head-butted Tony when he was eight years old. He knocked all of the teeth out of his head and taught him to take things the way they came. To be honest he was innocent in his own way. He grew up in a pig yard and Tony had to love him.

His told stories. His great, great aunt was the Countess Markievicz and she stood on the front line for the rising. They took half of her ear and she wouldn't talk or inform. It wasn't in her blood. She was a lady. Those women were in a league of their own hiding under floorboards, ringing bells to warn. They gave their lives and they never got enough recognition.

Tony picked his chin up off the ground to listen to those odes to Plunkett and Pearse. They kept him proud in the flats with his 10 brothers and sisters. The first one in the bed got the pillow. They had no blankets. They wrapped their coats around their shivers and Tony took two pots to the soup kitchen in the evenings. He got their dinners there and all of the people in the place knew Tony.

He was a little gent. Two of his brothers had paralysis and his parents got a red-bricked house to take better care of them. His mother lit a little red candle for them every evening. The little light would frighten the big shadows away and things were looking up. There was a park not too far from their house and Tony's mother would bring the children there on Sundays. They brought their sandwiches and bought ice-creams.

They were dog poor. The same as every one else. Tony was an average boy with average dreams of money and cars back then.

All he wanted was to play cards and football, cowboys and indians. Those years were precious. They were torches in the barren bowls of the city, junk, joints and guts of life. They made grown men fall to their knees in the streets, praying, stuttering gibberish and Tony held onto them in that dark hour.

He caught himself between dreaming, sleeping and sweating. His eyeballs were loose cannons and his body was lurching forward. He knew one step, two steps was all it would take to kill the rotten vermin and stop it from chewing his bones clean. He nudged his head through the widening crook of the noose and he was floating, swaying, nauseous. His torso was throbbing, from days and endless nights on couches, park benches and bloodied floors.

He was dying. It had been three days since his last hit and the cold turkey was wringing him dry. The rat would certainly eat the rest. It was greedy and without morals or compassion. It didn't give a damn about Tony and his face like a ticking clock. The doctors weren't any better. They told him he had no more veins, no more chances in his arms and asked him questions about his heart.

It was routine.

They never truly believed he had one. They'd seen the tracks, the records and most people were afraid of him. They crossed the street to get away from him and he couldn't blame them. He didn't want to be near him either. He sighed and wondered what they

whispered, what they made of his wretched turmoil. But it didn't matter anymore and it never really mattered in the beginning. All they saw were their impressions from the other side of the kerb and the maggots of his flesh, crawling and gnawing at him.

His breath shortened and he remembered the city, the highs, red-eyed midnight tea – and the madness that spurred the laughter, the hiccups, the sex and Genesis. He cried for the beauty of the streets and the people in its trolleys hitting lows. He was hollow and gasping, parching, dying three times and resurrecting in puddles of his own piss. He was dragged, beaten and beating, robbed and robbing and thrown to the gallows of the never ending traffic of syringes and night to stumble home and find out he didn't live there anymore.

He filled the holes with needles. That rat was a bastard; Tony didn't stand a chance against it. He stopped going to school when he was 11 years old. The school authorities sent him down the country to a school for students with bad behaviour and the priests were well-dressed fiends. They had the boys tortured and there was one horrible looking bloke that used to linger on the edge of Tony's bed with his hand sneaking along the white linen. Tony stuck a fork in the side of his face one night.

He gripped the sheets for his dear, dwindling life and the priests threw him in a padded cell after that. They didn't believe him. The other boys knew too well and told Tony to scream when it happened again. They banged their bed pots to keep him safe and showed him how to sniff out the weasels.

He went home a couple of weeks later. He told his mother what happened and she took him to the doctor. Penetrated, he said and Tony got a few bob for the trouble and for keeping quiet. His mother let him leave school and got him a job as a van boy. He brought the bread to the door and got a £10 note every week. He split it with his mother and gave his father a pound for his empty pocket.

He found a rat in his back garden, rustling in the rubbish and scouring for something to sink its filthy fangs into. He killed it and walked out of his house to haunt the cobbles in his rebellion. He didn't want to be there. He was tired of pretending. His parents were still talking about the ladies and the gentlemen while his father threw digs. His mother tried to save Tony from the hellish darkness outside the door.

There were plenty of rats. He saw them running along the canal, climbing walls, stalls and dragging their tails behind them. They were pests. Tony couldn't get away from them. He was out all the time, meeting the lads under the dripping of archways and stars. He was having a laugh and drinking two flagons of cider before the night went out. He chuckled home, fell asleep and got up to pick magic mushrooms on the Curragh. He brought home bags of them and brewed them up with tea.

The giggling was insant.

He was out of it. Laughing. He sold handfuls of them for a fiver and went to the hospital for smiling and grinding his teeth. He was taking LSD and dissolving into the streets week in, week out. They were all out of their heads, singing, flashing, dancing under the halos of the moon. They were free from the barbed wire cage of reality and scraping through the day with the rats, none of them wanted to go home.

Tony was sitting by the dock with his mate who had a couple of ounces of cocaine. Tony hadn't heard of it before and he sniffed the white line of powder off the packet of Major. He was on top of the world. For a while, he was buzzing and every week was just the same, until it was more and more and he couldn't stop.

He was in and out of work, people's purses and homes, thieving, feeding his habit. There was a lad called Lenny with acne and old man's blood in his veins. He was Tony's partner in crime.

They did everything together. They saw the people strung out on heroin in the bars and something on their faces that resembled a bit of happiness. They wanted to try it and it cost them a fiver for their first hit. They stuck it up their noses and shared the bag, the highs, the lows and their needles.

Tony had a fake identity, a moustache and a pair of George Webb shoes, skintight Wrangler jeans and a Ben Sherman shirt, a Wrangler jacket. The chicks were dripping for him like honey and all of the locals knew him. They would sneak him pints of Harp and ask him about his parents. But he didn't talk to them very much. He had nothing he wanted to say or hear and he was busy making a despicable creature out of himself.

He was in bits. He had a cold. It was the sickness. Lenny told him it was the withdrawals and he was right. Tony bought another score and felt fine. He was hooked and sniffing two bags a week, swallowing tiny armies of valium to dream. He signed himself into a clinic. He was 17 and only there for a few weeks. His mother left his cigarettes at the door and the doctors got him clean. But they barely fed him and they were asking him about his private thoughts.

He waited until the ward echoed with their snores and jumped out of the window and onto the moon of light on the pavement. He walked home and they were there, standing by his driveway. His mother said, come in son and slammed the door on them.

She wouldn't turn him away.

He stopped using and dodged the bullet, kicked his heels and got work tiling ceilings, sweeping roads. He let the months pass in their dreary stride and tried it again. Once a week, he told himself. But it was Friday, Saturday, Sunday and back to the clinic. He got clean, dirty, clean, dirty and showed his face around all the old spots. The rats were running riot and he was putting £20 worth of heroin up his nose a night.

It did nothing.

He needed a needle the man said before knotting the turnkey and finding the vein, shoving it in. Take that out. Take it out, Tony roared. He only had half of the gear in his arm and he felt like he was gone, perished and rising from the ashes of it all to roll a cigarette. He was doped out of his mind and sitting, sleeping in different alleyways and flats with different rats and the TV blinking with static. He passed out and woke up to find one of them munching at his shoelace.

He was disgusted.

He could feel its tail licking the hairs of his leg and he was sure another must have scraped its way through to the drains of his veins. He was so high. He couldn't get up to go to the toilet or tell if there was a bit of himself left inside the gutters of his limbs. He'd turned it on and he was chasing it round and round, trying to get that hit. He robbed hospitals and hopped over counters with a plastic gun. He was buying and forging prescriptions for £20 and 60 Dycanol, another trip.

He sold the rest to get more. He slept with knives.

He fell in love with his blue-eyed turtle dove, Imelda. She was stunning. They were eyeing each other up all night and Tony asked her if she wanted a go. She did and that was it for a year. They played family in her apartment with her daughter. Tony did all of the cooking and the cleaning. He tattooed her name on his arm and found her shooting up in bed and pulling her knickers down in a bush. She was on the game, selling herself to light up and they were engaged.

Tony left. He was barely in the door of his parents' house when he was dragged back out. He got 18 months in the 'Joy for armed robbery and he had to stand up and be counted in there. The rats took anything they got their filthy hands on and Tony made knives out of razor blades and batons out of batteries dropped into socks.

He was stabbed by a bloke in the corridor one evening. Tony stuck his finger in the fella's eye and he thought he'd killed him stone dead. But he took the eyeball clean out instead. Two lifers jumped in and broke it up while the screws watched and witnessed. They told the court it was self-defence, Tony hadn't done anything wrong. He was innocent and it was the itinerants that saved him that day.

Tony stuck with them. They were his family and they shared their cells, their rollies. The rat was devouring his brains, crunching, chomping. There was blood ringing in his ears and the words, life is a cabaret old friend mocked him to sleep in his cell. It was what he used to say before the gear got him down on his knees.

He had a £100 when he got out of the 'Joy and he spent more money on the taxi than he did on the gear. Two weeks later, he was strung out and squatting in a flat with his skin flaking off from the bleach and the head-lice. There were children everywhere screaming and he couldn't go home – not that time. He had to stay there and rot away with the rat molesting his soul. He got up one morning and thought he had left enough for another hit, but he hadn't. He went cold turkey for three days. The rat tormented his brain and he couldn't sleep. He lay awake contemplating his life, his choices and death. He tied the noose and two steps was all it took to hang the rat, the hell, the gentleman and leave him dangling, waiting for heaven.

❈   ❈   ❈

The beam broke and the slight corpse of his body shuttled across the concrete, lugging the trapped air from his lungs. His luck petrified him in the darkness. The door opened and white light shone upon the rags of his gentle heartbeats as he was picked from the filth.

A rat scuttled out and down the hall. Tony thanked God. Every day. His buddy found him and took him to the hospital where he stayed for a few weeks and got on a maintenance programme. He was on methadone for life and lived in a small flat his welfare could afford. He picked at the memory of those words his mother spoke when he was a child and gave his bloods once a week. He saw the shrink and tried to sand down the hardened welts of the years.

He just wanted to be clean. Respectable. He hadn't seen his family in months. They didn't trust him enough. But now he was different. His mind was clear and he wasn't crying or itching and looking to score. He had a chance for the first time in his life. He used his manners to make something of himself and decorated his place, kept it clean. He was a top tenant.

His landlord drove him to the hospital for his meetings and he was sorry to see Tony go when his mother showed up on his doorstep crying. She was proud of what he'd done but it was time for him to go home. He was chuffed. There was a new bed in his room and a sign painted on the wall.

'Welcome home, son.'

He'd made it.

A year and a half later, he got the key for the front door. He was trusted and shaking in a flitter of tears. He was giving blood down at the huts. He collapsed, blacked out and woke up in a hospital unit with a mask on and machines flashing and bleeping beside him.

He couldn't remember his name or the alphabet and it was the HIV, the doctors told him. His mother would take care of him. She'd sent off to America for literature. She was a step ahead of the posse and she helped Tony understand the sickness. It was the rat, it was a death sentence and Tony took it on the chin.

He was lucky. He was still alive.

He got his hair cut and got up, swept the floor and tidied up after himself. The boss was impressed and he offered Tony a job keeping the place tidy. There were to be no drugs and no messing, one chance and one chance only. Tony never let him down. He was there for 20 years. The customers loved him and the boss trusted him with the money.

They were mates. The boss got a divorce, hung a note on his door telling Tony to call the police and he did. It broke another piece of his jigsaw heart. He didn't just lose a boss, he lost a friend and the world lost another of its gentlemen. His father had died too. Years before he told Tony that he was proud of him. He wasn't taking those injections anymore. He was clean and he knew it. He had no doubt about it or the future. He was still living with his mother in that red-brick house.

She was his rock. He took of care of her. She was frail and she couldn't get around the house as well as she used to. She needed Tony to change her sheets, make her dinner and wash her up for bed. He tucked her in and blew out the candles that kept the darkness at bay. He was happy to. He kept to himself most of the time. He crossed the street when he saw the red-eyed remnants of the past.

The junkies. He hated that word. It cut him like a knife and left his wounds open for the picking. There was no need for it, he said. His old friend, Lenny rang him up every now and then. He asked Tony for a score and Tony gave it to him. He couldn't change him. It was the thing about living with the rats. They maul everything and bury their illnesses closer to the bone than the marrow.

They were hard to see from the inside.

Tony keeps himself clean and people tell him, he's looking good, In fact, he had become the perfect gentleman that his mother asked him to be.

14 On The Fairy Trail

ELAINE'S MOTHER told her about the fairies. They lived at the bottom of the garden and they had little wings and puckered ears. Her mother talked to them through the thorns and told Elaine she was going to have to throw out the rain to find them. They were somewhere and Elaine believed in them more than anything. She trusted her mother and tore up the dirt every day looking for the fairies.

She never found them.

Her mother took her everywhere and Elaine thought that if she paid enough attention to her mother, she could be like her and talk to them. Her mother was an awful woman for talking. She was always chatting to people in the streets and nattering away to Elaine's grandmother.

Her mother liked to visit her a couple of times a week and Elaine sat on her mother's lap and listened up, not a word was to be missed while her mother was there.

She talked about the night she met Elaine's father at a party and how she would have rambled on if he hadn't stopped her and caught her like a ribbon between his teeth. They were married in 1978. Elaine's mother never liked the city and they bought a house in the country. Her mother had a garden and her father had enough just knowing she was happy.

He liked to make her laugh.

He told Elaine's mother ridiculous things and she always believed him and laughed with him. He was exhausted. He worked every day of the week and the grit of labour had left nothing of his nerves or his temper. He would be roaring and screaming and all Elaine's mother had to do was wave her hand to calm him down.

He was a worrier.

Elaine loved him.

He played with her and stood her up on his shoulders to have a look for the fairies. He'd never seen them either. But he told her he believed in them and helped her dress up as one for halloween. She usually went as a witch with her mother and her sister, Danielle. She was five years older than Elaine and Halloween was her favourite time of year.

It was Elaine's too.

And her mother's.

They went all out for it and covered the house in cotton webs and plastic skeletons. Her mother kept a broom under the stairs and sent Elaine to a Montessori hippy kind of school. They were heavy on the arts and crafts and there was no religion.

Elaine's mother had gone to school with the nuns and she didn't want Elaine putting up with the same abuse. The nuns caned her for talking and the teachers told Elaine to keep it down. She was always doing impressions and comedy sketches for the class.

She was a hoot. She told all of her classmates about the fairies and how her mother could talk to them.

Her mother was always around, somewhere, doing something and Elaine hated to see her go anywhere without her. She would shower the sheets of her cheeks every time her mother left. Tears fell like jelly from her lashes and her shoulders hiccupped until her mother came home.

She took care of Elaine when she was sick. She rented videos for her, bought fizzy cola and rubbed her cheeks with her cold, cold hands. She held the earth in place and Elaine couldn't imagine a day without her. She was eight years old and she didn't understand what was going on.

Her mother had been fundraising for years for charity but the shocking news about Chernobyl and the children of Belarus and moved her in a special way. She had the house filled with boxes of toilet rolls and children's shoes, baby clothes, raffle supplies, long-life food packs and black sacks full of lollipops they wouldn't allow through the Ukrainian border. She organised aid convoys and brought dentists, electricians and carpenters to go over there and work for free.

Elaine wished she wouldn't. She sat on her mother's bed and watched her pack her suitcase for the children. She asked her when she was going to be back and her mother promised she would be home before Elaine knew it.

She was right. She was showing Elaine the pictures she took of the place and the yellow walls she painted, the plants she potted and the lovely people she met. She told Elaine she had to keep going over there. The children needed her more than anything. Elaine had to let her go and she couldn't even cry when her mother left every couple of weeks to try to smuggle health care across the border.

It meant too much to her. She explained how a nuclear plant over there had melted and exploded. The smoke blistered the sky and the people's skin resulting in thousands of them getting cancer. Birds dropped dead out of trees and afterwards children were born with deformities and brain damage.

Her mother was standing in the middle of every photograph. Her arms were entangled in the arms, shoulders and shaved heads of the smiling children and her hair was cut short. She'd dyed it purple or pink and she was wearing all of her jewellery. There was never anything dull about her as she made sure children had childhoods and schoolbooks because of her.

Elaine was 11 years old when she stopped looking for the fairies. Her grandmother was in hospital and her mother had told her to write a letter but not to write 'get well soon.' Her grandmother wasn't getting better and her mother was very honest about it even though she was devastated. As it happened Elaine's grandmother died when her mother was in Belarus and she came home straight away.

She said her goodbyes, made her peace and organised the wreaths. She wrote: 'Thanks for everything, Mam,' on the piece of card she put inside the bouquet of flowers.

Elaine used to look everywhere for the fairies but when she saw her grandmother resting, stiff in that wooden box, she wasn't sure she wanted to dig up the dirt anymore.

Her grandmother was underneath it. She figured it was best to forget about the fairies. She was growing up and her parents were fighting more and more. They didn't need another uprooting. Elaine's father moved out in 2000. She watched him reverse down the driveway and pull off in a cyclone of dust and smoke and she was glad of it in one way. It meant her parents couldn't argue and she could concentrate on the other miscellaneous threads of her youth.

Her parents needed space from each other but she got to see her father all the time. Elaine would hear her mother crying sometimes. She crawled up onto the bed beside her to hug her. They talked but Elaine found that something had changed in her mother. She had no more time for nonsense or other people's charred opinions.

Life was too short to prevaricate, she said.

Even so, she allowed Elaine's father to move back home, and their relationship improved on the new footing. By then Elaine had grown into a typical teenager. She was telling her parents to shut up and arguing over clothes. Her mother caught her drinking when she was13. She wasn't angry but she talked to Elaine about it.

She asked her if it was because of everything that happened with her father and Elaine nodded. She didn't want to tell her mother that she was just being a stupid teenager. She didn't want to worry her. She was getting in trouble in school for talking and dyeing her hair and she perfected her mother's signature to get away with it.

Her mother always had different people doing different bits and pieces around the house. There was a Romanian woman that washed the dishes and a lady from the Philippines who dusted the mantle and the presses. Nobody would ever hire them except her mother who would give them some money for their children, the bit of work they might have done and drop them home into the bargain.

She had children from Belarus come to stay with them every summer. There were also teachers, translators and doctors and they would be running out of beds by the end of it. There was Andy who her mother found praying on the porch in the middle of the night. She gave him a blanket to sleep on the porch.

He was mad but he was nice.

Elaine sat and had breakfast with him before he left. She realised she was more like her mother than she thought and the older she got, the more she seemed to look like her too. They laughed about it. Elaine was wearing her mother's leather boots and her amber rings, her dangly earrings. When it came to the Leaving Cert she just went in and did it and got jobs in music stores, phone stores and video rental stores after it.

Once sitting on her mother's bed, she went through the boxes and boxes of photographs. Polaroids and reels of film her mother had stacked underneath her wax jacket in her wardrobe. She had pictures and short film clips of herself when she was younger at the beach building sand castles and jumping waves.

She hadn't changed. She was listening to Elaine talk about her future and Elaine was thinking that maybe she could be a photographer. But she wasn't sure. She didn't think she had the eye for it. Her mother trusted Elaine and would share those photographs, those moments with her and that made up Elaine's mind.

She spent a year doing a portfolio course and applied to do photography in the city when she finished. She didn't get in and her mother told her not to worry and to try again next year. Elaine did and she got in that time. She brought her camera everywhere and saved up enough money to buy better quality cameras. She was trying to capture something very specific and she didn't know what it was.

Her mother continued to travel back and forth to Belarus. She was more and more involved in the children's lives and their communities and Elaine wanted to photograph the children. She asked her mother to buy her a plane ticket to Belarus for her 21st birthday. Her mother took her to visit some friends the night they arrived. They got quite merry to say the least.

The camera snapped and Elaine's mother caught the two of them crusty-eyed with sleep and lying, entwining in the same single bed of a Belarussian home the next morning. They were pale and sick from the vodka and the biscuits that were put in front of them all night.

They went to see the children in the orphanage every day Elaine was there. Her mother held her tears tight and remembered the hooves that had kicked out the dirt of her heart the first time she saw those children. She cried too and helped them organise their bits of glitter for Elaine's birthday party. They drew pictures and spelled their words as best they could.

They cheered her up. They recognised her from the photograph her mother kept of her and her sister in her purse and they held her hand. They were beautiful. They had celestial eyes and swollen heads and the poverty they endured sunk its hooks into the flesh of Elaine's affection.

Her mother got really sick in Belarus. She blacked out and stayed in bed for a week when she got home. Elaine's father took her to the hospital and they thought it was her sinuses. She had to stay there for the night and the next few after that. Elaine went to visit her with her sister. Her father was sleeping in there and all three of them were standing around her, talking and interrupting each other.

Her mother was wearing sunglasses to stop the light hurting her eyes and raising her hand to speak. She was still the same and telling the girls to go home. There was no need for them to spend the night. Elaine gave her a hug and a kiss and left and went back to say, 'I love you.'

Their father told them he'd only been out of the room for a second and their mother had buckled, died and been resuscitated, stabilised. They had to be there. The doctor was standing over her, pumping air in and out of her lungs and explaining everything, the brain haemorrhage and the strokes.

Her mother was getting less and less responsive and every day was a different hope, a different fear in the yellow inferno of the family room. Elaine played cards with her father and her sister in there. She watched telly, made jokes and pointless phone calls. She washed their hands everywhere they went. She wore her mother's rings and when she held her mother's hand, it looked as if she was holding her own.

Her mother was in hospital for three weeks and hadn't improved. The doctors couldn't lie to Elaine or her father or her sister. Her mother wasn't getting better and Elaine was legging it outside to get sick all over that sunny day.

She couldn't breath.

She had a dream about her mother that night. Her mother sat up in the hospital bed, pulled the mask from her face and said, she had to go, she had to go. That's all she kept saying. She had to go. But go where? Gone? That was all the doctors said, dressed in their white cloaks. They had lost her just as if the fairy light inside of her had been put out.

Elaine would only ever see her again a silhouette in the waking doorways of twilight and dreams. All of her mother's brain activity ceased on that Tuesday morning, two days before Elaine's 23rd birthday.

She turned off the engine, pulled the key from the ignition and made her way towards the front door of her house. She hadn't been there in weeks or since the funeral and the people came and told her stories and things about her mother that she'd never heard before. Her mother never mentioned them. She just did them and Elaine thought that if she looked hard enough and poured out her tears, she would find her mother.

She was screaming, scraping the grief up off the floor of her gut and walking around her house. She needed to talk to her mother and tell her that she needed her.

Her mother would have wanted her to stop and take a deep breath. She was the image of her mother and beginning to feel more and more like her every day. She knew what her mother would say in that mammy way that keeps the moon going round in circles and the faces of sunflowers looking up.

"Elaine honey, don't worry."

She could undo the entire world and nothing would change. Her mother's scent would still cling to the wax jacket hanging in her wardrobe and the boxes of photographs and films would still be there. Elaine needed them for her final project in college. Her mother was her inspiration and Elaine had never taken her photograph.

She never thought of it.

Imagine.

She put one of the films on and the white light beamed against the wall. Her mother was a small girl, burying herself into the lap of the ocean. She was spinning round and round on the merry-go-round. She was spun from time entirely.

She couldn't be gone. She never left the places she loved. She spilt over them like wax off a candle and sunk her soft skin into the creases, the cracks. Elaine smiled and covered the floor and the furniture with her mother's photographs. She found pictures of her mother's first steps, her communion and her trips to the forests and the parks. The hairs prickled on Elaine's arms like the charge of a billion, boundless fairy feet.

Her mother was everywhere and she knew for sure she would never be far away from her.

15 The Campervan Blues

CILLIAN'S PARENTS bought the campervan the year he was born. They made a promise to make things better at home and take the campervan all over Ireland and to England or France maybe. They were fighting all of time at that stage of their marriage and were taking it in turns to pack their bags, go and come back saying 'sorry'.

They couldn't stop.

They would tell the children to go to bed, close their doors and their curtains before the night had shovelled out what was left of the day. They knew they had let them down, time and again. They tried keeping it from them and fixing what was broken with less and less success.

Then Cillian came along.

His heartbeat filled the hospital room and his parents drew the same astounded breath and traced the white spaceship of his head with their fingers on the computer screen. He was an angel or an alien hitching a ride with his weird white thumb in the womb. He was a sonic boom that was due any day and they were ready to wipe the red blubbery lining from his crown and kiss the Hallelujah of his soft, pink skin.

He was born 7lb 6oz.

He took up all of their time and their words with his nappies and his bottles. He managed to get the whole family together to watch him splashing in the kitchen sink. Laughing wildly with the pure and utter joy, he bounced and picked himself up off the ground after learning how to walk.

They took special care of him.

They wanted to.

The children got up before school to feed him. His father went straight out to work in his digger in the morning. He worked busy days but tried to get home earlier in the evenings to be with him.

He made renewed efforts to hold his tongue and his temper. His wife cooked the dinner, filed the accounts, the kitchen towels and new thoughts of what might be.

They were just like every other parents.

They weren't perfect.

They had a house in the middle of the mountains. They had an acre of land for the children to distract themselves in with a tree house and an Alsatian named King. He kept them safe and barked at the birds a lot of the time. He stayed in the yard with Cillian's father as he worked on the engines and machines down there. Cillian's father was the best. He was good with cars and always helping someone or anyone who asked.

He gave them a chance.

Both of his parents were alcoholics and he never got as much as a kiss when he was younger. He reared himself. He scavenged for his own food, picked the branches for his own beatings and scorned himself into sleeplessness.

Cillian's mother didn't mind the cleaning or the gardening. She liked to be busy and up before the dawn, rushing around to get the children ready to catch the school bus. She was a full-time mother and the hand that fed the crying mouth at midnight with Calpol and sweeter dreams.

She took the children rollerblading in the park and picking apples from the trees she had growing in the garden to bake them apple pie. She used the recipe her mother gave her and told Cillian all about her parents, the poverty and their trips to Cork and

Kerry for picnics in the fields and splashing contests on the rocks of the sea with her sisters. That was then.

Now the campervan was going to pot down there in the corner where his parents left it. Cillian couldn't leave it alone. He had a mission to make it right. He wasn't afraid to go inside the crusty thing. His older brother and sisters had left school, moved out and bought tickets to Australia and New Zealand. It was just Cillian in the house with his parents who, as he grew older, had found the time and the words to start arguing all over again.

They dragged up each and every corpse of a memory they'd ever condemned to the dirt of their forgiveness and allowed it resurrect itself more painfully than the last time it had seen the light of the same sorrow. They called each other this and that, put themselves to sleep in separate beds after they'd tired themselves out good and proper.

They never listened to Cillian.

He looked up to them with his eyes blue and clear as his innocence. He kept saying, 'stop it, stop it, stop it!' until they bit at the blind frustration in his voice and sent him outside to play in the garden. They could see him every once in a while looking under the rocks and shooting the plastic guns they'd given him to keep him quiet.

He was happy enough.

He had a secret.

He'd been cleaning out the campervan and taking things from the kitchen and his bedroom. He was doing it up, making himself a hut. He forgot how long he'd been working on it one day. He was in his own wonderful world and he hadn't heard his mother yelling at him from the house. His parents walked out and around looking for him and calling his name. They went down to the yard and saw the door of the unvarnished campervan swinging stiffly on its hinges.

Cillian was a gift really.

There he was playing with his father's tools and the teddy bear his mother had sewn back up when they found him. His parents couldn't give out to him. He'd done a good tidying up job and reminded his parents that they hadn't delivered on their promise to do up the campervan so that they could take holidays in it.

Again they promised that they were going to strip off the paint, sand down the rust and take it wherever they pleased.

His father took time off work to work on it and his mother helped clean it up and then pack his Nintendo and the tent she had bought and shown him how to pitch in the garden. He could sleep with the stars, she told him. They were out of the house by noon. They had their smiles and their seat belts on.

His father turned the key in the ignition and it started for a second. They held the hope in their breath while the campervan rumbled and trembled itself back into a useless coma. Cillian's mother shouted at his father to sort it out. Cillian stayed with his father helping him to try to fix the engine until the day had to give up on the night.

His mother brought them tea.

It was no use.

It was dead.

His parents couldn't afford a new engine to put into it and Cillian looked at it in a flush of warm fury. He started screaming at the campervan, his ticket to a dream.

He was sick of it, sick of watching it go to pieces. He couldn't look at it anymore. His cheeks were throbbing and his ears were burning with the noise of his parents emptying it out and spitting their rotten words at each other.

They hadn't seen the tears or the disappointment on his face. They were trapped in their own troubles and Cillian was a quick, wet flurry getting out of there. He grabbed his father's fireworks and threw the bag he'd packed over his shoulder. He ran as hard and as fast he could into the dark dungeons of the forest outside his gate and his parents hardly heard the gravel cracking underneath his feet.

He was running away and reefing himself up the rocks, over tree stumps and through the thorny barbs of the bushes. His head was full. He couldn't feel the hot scrapes of pain anymore. He stopped running and stood still at the top of the mountain. The city was shining louder and more ferociously than any firework he had ever seen. He dropped everything in his hands, head and heart and poured out the contents of his bag. He started pitching the tent and waiting for his parents to come around.

He could hear them shouting.

Cillian.

Cillian.

They were scouting around with their flashlights looking for him and blaming each other. They never gave it up. They were a ghastly babble in the tightening distance. Their cries were enormous and torrential but then they stopped when the spotted him in the distance. They watched him construct the poles, hang the waterproof fabric and work diligently under the disco light of the moon.

It was peaceful.

Cillian's parents hid behind trees and listened as he talked to himself about the size of sky. He was done stabbing the tent poles into the dirt when his mother walked over to sit beside him. Cillian hugged her. He was glad to see her. He wanted to ask her if he could stay there for the night.

She said she would have to wait until his father got back. They sat in a communion of silence which was peaceful until a terrible thunder growled its way towards them in the mountain. There were lights poking their white fingers between the branches. There was a roar of a beastly engine heaving its thick petrol pipes up the cliff and arriving at the foot of the clearing like a lighted UFO.

It was his father in his digger with the campervan being dragged along. It was chained to the digger, his father parked it up, folded out three chairs under its awning and said they would live the dream under the stars as they slept up there for the night.

Cillian's parents held hands and smiled at each other. They had honoured that old promise in some way and it was enough for them to know that they would do it again when they got the new engine for the campervan.

Tonight though had its own compensations and that would do for now.

Cillian was on top of the world.

NOTES

NOTES

~ ACKNOWLEDGEMENTS ~

I WOULD like to thank each of the people I interviewed for allowing me into their homes, their lives, their minds and their memories. I am sincerely grateful for the truth they shared with me and I have them to thank for the honesty in these pages.

They are my heroes.

I want to thank my editor, PJ Cunningham for all his encouragement and his time, his suggestions, his patience and his belief, and my mother and my father for their support and the wonderful way they are.

Thanks is due to Kevin Morgan and Anna Morgan for the cover photograph and cheers to the many strangers, poets, artists and pedestrians that stopped to answer my wandering questions.

I would also like to praise my friends and salute them for putting up with me, listening to me and consoling my many whims.

I would also like to praise Eimear Doyle and Jessica (Jess) Sullivan and salute them for putting up with me, listening to me and consoling my many whims. My friends, Lisa Keegan, Amy Plant, Sarahlee Madigan, Jade Dillon, Sophie Rigney, Aoife Mannion, Louise Fletcher, Fintan Duffy Rice, Richard Timmy Berger and anyone and everyone I may have forgotten or who has lent me their ear.

Aoife Caffrey, I am in your debt for the profile picture, the long nights, the long interpretations and the fears you put to rest.

Finally, Mark Cummins, I love your sense of sense.

I thank you all beyond my words.

~ ABOUT THE AUTHOR ~

The Tell Tale Collection is Maeve Devoy's first book. Maeve (23) is a journalism graduate from Dublin City University and since she left college in 2011, she has been interviewing people from all over Ireland and collecting their life stories.